SONG TITLE SERIES

ABBA

JOAN MAGUIRE

Copyright Page

New: ABBA

Author: Joan Maguire

National Library of Australia Cataloguing-in-Publication – Publication entry

Creator:	Maguire, Joan, author
Title:	ABBA / Joan Maguire.
ISBN:	978-0-9941998-1-2 (paperback)
Series:	Song title series.
Notes:	Includes bibliography references
Subjects	Family vacations--Fiction
	Natural Disasters--Fiction
	Titles of musical compositions--Fiction

Dewey Number: A823. 4

Published with the assistance of CreateSpace and is available through the Print on Demand Network or www.songtitleseries.com

This soft cover short story book was created and written
By Joan Maguire on14th November 2012 ©
ISBN: 978-0-9941998-1-2

E-book re-written April 2014©
EISBN: 978-0-9925964-6-0

This book was converted into large print in March 2015 © and is available through the same distributors as the normal book or
www.songtitleseries.com
ISBN: 978-0-9943297-5-2 (large print)

DEDICATION

I would like to dedicate this book and say to thank you to my Earth Angel David and his friends, who inspire and motivate me to achieve things that I never dreamt, were possible.

INTRODUCTION

Legally I cannot use Lyrics or Music because of Copyright but I can use song titles so a total of 742 song titles (Italicized) have been used to make the following story possible. Also due to the nature of my books; legally I must place a Reference (exactly the way it is down loaded) and Bibliography in the back of the book.

Three families from three different countries all go to an Adventure Park in Europe for a holiday. They are brought together by their children playing in the playground. Join the families as they enjoy each others company and learn about the different issues that a family can have.

Follow the story of the unusual last week of their holidays and how each family deals with the message from each child that was given to them by one of two strange but identical looking men, an unexpected natural disaster that occurs in the middle of the week and the unexplainable healings of life threatening injuries. See how the families rally around each other in their time of need and what can happen if you trust one another.

See if you can work out who the stranger is and did he really heal the people who should have died through their injuries?

When reading this "Song Title Series" book, I hope that no disservice has been done to ABBA as well as their adoring fans who read it, for that was not my intention. As I may have missed a song, an album or a concert within this book I do apologize sincerely. I have created and written this story without the sanctity of ABBA and I hope that if they read this they will enjoy it as well.

Well sit back and enjoy the story and don't forget that because of using the original song titles in whole, there are places in the book that I could not change to make it more comprehensible for you the reader.

ACKNOWLEDGEMENTS

I would like to thank my daughters, Jenny and Kylie for their positive but critical input in the first draft of this book and all the help and support that they have given me throughout the Song Title Series books. With taking their input to mind, I have improved the book.

I would also like to thank my son Peter and his family for their support and help in keeping me grounded.

I would like to thank Kay and Julie for their patience and understanding whilst teaching me and giving me the skills to present my unique books in the best way possible.

I would also like to thank my good friend Tim for his generosity in supplying me with an original photo of the Swiss Alps for the cover.

I would like to thank The First 24 Hour Foundation for supplying me with the information on disaster plans and risk management.

I would like to thank everyone else who has helped me bring this book to life and to you for purchasing it.

OTHER BOOKS IN THE SONG TITLE SERIES

Bon Jovi – Wanted Dead Or Alive
Green Day
AC/DC
Beach Boys
Slim Dusty
Country Women
Five Country Men
Six Crooners
Three crooners
ABBA
The Rat Pack
Elton John
Classic 50s & 60s Rock 'N' Roll

CONTENTS

MAKING NEW FRIENDS

"*Fernando, Chiquitita;* lunch is ready." called their mother from the kitchen door.

"How are you going to explain the hole that you have in your pants? You know that mom will *go on and on and on* about it." said *Chiquitita* to her brother.

"I'll tell mom the truth. I'll tell her that I was *sitting in the palmtree* when I heard her calling and I accidentally tore them as I was coming down." said *Fernando*.

As the children sat down at the table, their mother asked "What have you two been up to this morning, besides ruining your clothes. I hope that you two enjoy yourselves this year because it could be *our last summer* here at the *Waterloo* Holiday Adventure Park. Nina has been helping me and I think that Hasta has been reading in his room."

Their father came in through the front door and sat at the table beside his youngest twin children and said "It would be nice if you took your brother and sister with you to the playground this afternoon. The weather is too nice for them to stay inside all day."

"But dad, *Hasta Manana* keeps running away and he gets us into trouble." griped *Fernando*.

His father said "*He is your brother* so keep a closer eye on him and if he keeps running off, then come and get *one of us* to bring him home. Nina, when you go out, *put on your white sombrero* and don't lose it again."

After lunch was finished, the children wandered down towards the playground and saw *one man, one woman* and another young girl banging something on the ground before they threw it into the air. Whatever they were throwing came back to them and they caught it.

Curiosity got the better of the children so they went over to see what the other people were doing. The children stood watching for a few minutes, and then *Fernando* asked "What are you doing? What is that thing that you are banging, before throwing and catching it?"

The young girl replied "This is a different boomerang to what we usually throw and we *bang-a-boomerang* on the ground before we throw it, so it will come back to us.

Would you like to try throwing and catching one? It's not hard once you've learnt how to do it."

Hasta Manana said "I don't know if we should. *My mama said* that we shouldn't talk to strangers."

"Your mother is right." said the young girl "my name is *Cassandra* and these are my parents. We learnt to *bang-a-boomerang* when we were visiting Australia. I wanted to come and *bang-a-boomerang* this afternoon but I am not allowed to do it unless my parents are with me because it can be dangerous. We do it differently than *the way the old friends* do it, back in Australia, but it's still fun. Now would you like to try it?"

"One of us will go and ask our parents if it is alright with them first." said *Fernando*.

"I'll go." said *Chiquitita* and started running back towards the lodge that the family had rented for their holiday.

As she reached the door of the lodge, her father was coming out and asked "Has *Hasta Manana* run off again?"

"No." said *Chiquitita* "there's *one man, one woman* and a girl named *Cassandra* down near the park and they *bang-a-boomerang* on the ground before throwing and catching it. They would like to teach us how to do it, but I thought that I had better come and ask you first, if it was alright. You can come and learn too dad, if you want to and mom if she isn't busy."

"That sounds interesting and fun. *I wonder* if your mother would like to come along as well. Wait a moment while I go and ask her." said her father.

Her father came back outside a few minutes later and said "Let's go. Your mother will be down as soon as she's finished what she's doing."

When they reached the place near the playground where the others were, *Cassandra* showed them what to do.

The first thing they learnt was, how to *bang-a-boomerang* properly, then they were shown the right way to hold the boomerang before throwing it. The funniest part was trying to throw it so it stayed in the air and the hardest part was learning to catch it when it came back.

"How *does your mother know* when to put her hands out to catch it? Every time I try to catch it, it keeps *slipping through my fingers*." said *Hasta Manana*.

"It takes a lot of practice and you have to keep your eye on the boomerang when it starts coming down as it's coming back to you. *The day before you came,* dad was in the championship in the *Summer Night City* men's finals for throwing and catching boomerangs and he won. *Al Andar* used to beat dad all the time and now *the king has lost his crown*." said *Cassandra*.

Then she added "*Al Andar* is one of those *soldiers* who serve with the *Super Trouper* Company and has done three tours of duty with them. The *Super Trouper* Company is the one who are immediately deployed to help when tragedy strikes; like a natural disaster. They help with search and rescue and then help with the rebuilding of the city or town. *When all is said and done,* they're givin' *a little bit more* of themselves to help other less fortunate people.

Not *so long* ago, the *Super Trouper* Company was sent to Asia when a tsunami hit many towns along the coast and a short way inland. For many of those *soldiers,* it was a case of *another train, another town* that needed their help. It was not a *happy New Year* for those people but with the company's *arrival,* to many people, it must have felt *like an angel passing through my room* or rather through their rooms with a *lovelight* to light their way out of the darkness that they had just been thrown into.

Looks like *mamma Mia* and dad are packing up for the day. I'll most probably come and *bang-a-boomerang* again tomorrow, if you want to try it again. We will be here at *Waterloo* for the next two weeks. The next time I see you, please call me Cassie." said *Cassandra*.

As Cassie and her family walked away, Nina said "*I wonder* why she calls her mother *mamma Mia?* I think that I'll ask her the next time I speak to her. Come on; let's go to the playground now, before we have to go home too."

Their dad said "Before you go, tell me *the name of the game* that you want to play tonight and I'll get it out. Nina, I think that it's your turn to choose the game."

"Let's play *Gimme! Gimme! Gimme!* I like taking all of *Hasta Manana's* chocolate from him because he always takes mine when we play *Under Attack*. That's a boy's game and I can't play it very well because *I am just a girl*." said Nina.

4

"No, you don't take all my chocolate." said *Hasta Manana*.

"Oh, yes *I do. I do, I do, I do, I do.*" said Nina teasingly to her brother.

At the playground, there were two new amusements for the children to play on. One was called "*On Top Of Old Smokey.*" and the other was called "*Ring Ring.*"

On Top Of Old Smokey was a climbing apparatus and an older child would have to climb a series of steps and ladders, both inside and outside of the structure to get to the top platform. It was not as easy as it looked.

Ring Ring was a lot easy to conquer as it was sets of rings lined up in different sizes that a younger child had to pick up and place on specific objects that would then become steps covered with rings as it wound its way up a small mound to a platform at the top. Unless the rings covering the objects were locked in place, a child could not use the steps to make their way up to the platform.

Nina's favorite ride was the *Merry-Go-Round* where she would ride the *tiger* she named *Dum Dum Diddle. Fernando* enjoyed the challenge of *On Top Of Old Smokey, Chiquitita* enjoyed listening to *Rikky Rock 'N' Roller,* the *rock 'n' roll band* that were rehearsing for the weekend picnic in the park gig.

Hasta Manana; well, he was just having fun going *head over heels* down the side of a small grassy mound and then walking funny. As he approached Nina, he would say "*I'm a marionette* and I'm coming to get you and take you to my hideout on my *eagle.*"

Nina would run to the *Merry-Go-Round* and jump on the *tiger* saying "Oh, no you're not. *Dum Dum Diddle* will protect me from your *eagle.*"

It was getting late and the children were starting to get hungry, so they headed back to the lodge. As they were passing by some tall bushes, *Chiquitita* thought that she saw Cassie hiding in them. She thought about going over to see if it was her but she didn't want the others going with her, so she didn't say anything.

Chiquitita couldn't get the thought of Cassie out of her head, so after the evening meal was finished and she had finished her chores, she snuck out to go and find her. She went back to the bushes and Cassie was still there hiding.

Cassie said "I saw you walking past and I know that you saw me hiding here. *I've been waiting for you* to come back because I need your help if you can give it to me? I want to run away to *Hamlet III,* it's a little town north, just past the *Waterloo* turn off. *My mama said* that if I wasn't happy, I could always go home.

Mamma Mia is my dad's second wife and they are always fighting over me. Dad is the *man in the middle* and I love him so much but I miss my real mother. *The day before you came,* they had a very big fight over me trying to take up too much of dad's time. *Why did it have to be me* that is the centre of their fights all the time when I'm with them?

I have a dream that I want to fulfil, but *mamma Mia* won't let me even talk about it; especially to dad. It makes me so angry sometimes when I try to talk to dad because she always interrupts us with "*Honey, Honey* can you please do this for me or *Honey, Honey* can you please go and get this for me. While you are gone, Cassie and I can do…whatever.

She always try to *disillusion* me and I think that all she's interested in is *money, money, money* and she's afraid that dad will spend some of his on me to fulfil my dream. She can keep the *money, money, money,* if that's what she wants. I only want to be able to talk to my dad without her butting in all the time. Will you help me get to *Hamlet III* tonight?"

"*Does your mother know* about what's going on and how you feel. I mean; your real mother. If my father finds out that I have snuck out, he'll go *on and on and on* about the dangers of being out alone at night. I know that *people need love* but I don't know how I can help you unless *one of us* talks to my mother. She'll know what to do. Will you come home with me and talk to her?" *Chiquitita* said.

Cassie said "Won't you get into trouble for being out at night?"

Chiquitita replied "Yes, I will but I'll just look at dad with my *angeleyes* and he'll soften. It always works, besides it's not as if I snuck out to be with a boy or to go to the *Summer Night City* dance.

Once you have spoken to my mother, she will not let him be angry with me for too long. *So long* as you explain to my mother what is happening at home and *so long* as it is the truth, then I doubt that I will get into trouble at all. Now, will you come with me?"

As the two girls walked through the back door, Nina said "You're in big trouble. Dad knows that you snuck out and he's been going *on and on and on* about it."

Chiquitita said "Nina, would you go and get mom please? Cassie, sit down and I'll get you a drink. Would you like a *SOS* cola or a *SOS* diet lemonade, a fruit juice or a glass of water?"

"A *SOS* cola please." said Cassie.

Chiquitita's mother came in and sat at the table with the girls. Cassie told her everything and apologized for getting *Chiquitita* into trouble.

"The first thing I think we'll do, is bring *Chiquitita*'s father in and get him to go over to your place Cassie and let your parents know that you're safe, and that you will be spending the night here with us. Tomorrow, after we have all had a good night's sleep; we'll try and work something out." *Chiquitita*'s mother said and then she looked at her daughter and continued saying "I'm not happy about you sneaking out, but under the circumstances, I think you can be excused. *When all is said and done,* if you hadn't gone to meet Cassie and if something had happened to her, then I would have been most disappointed in you for not doing something about it."

Nina yelled out "Are we going to play *Gimme! Gimme! Gimme!* tonight, because if we don't start soon, *Hasta Manana* will have eaten all of his chocolate and I won't be able to win them from him."

That evening Cassie got a taste of what it was like to have brothers and a sister and the noise and the competition while playing games and the little digs when *the winner takes it all;* all the chocolate that is. After the family had finished playing *Gimme! Gimme! Gimme!* they played a game of *Under Attack* before heading off to bed.

Cassie asked "Don't you ever get sick and tired of your brothers having digs at you all the time. At least I'm *free as a bumble bee* and I don't have to worry about anyone but myself.

When we were in Australia, *me and Bobby and Bobby's brother,* Brian, used to go fishing in the dam and he used to annoy me so much, that all I wanted to do was either, throw him in the dam or put him on the *midnight special* train to the Kimberley Ranges up north or to Alice Springs that was miles away inland; nearly to the middle of Australia."

Chiquitita replied "My brothers and my sister are *my love, my life* and I wouldn't want to lose any of them. Sure they can be a pain at times but *when all is said and done,* they can also be my saviour.

If I start feeling down, they are usually the ones that cheer me up. Sometimes, *I wonder, should I laugh or cry* when they act up but I usually end up doing both; they make me laugh till I cry. Unless you have brothers and sisters yourself, no one can explain what it is like having them. Haven't you at some time, wished that you had a brother or sister or both?"

Cassie thought for a moment, before saying "Yes, I have thought about it, quite a few times actually; but what I have been through over these past few years, I'm glad that I'm the only child.

Thank you for being there for me today, especially as you only met me briefly this afternoon. It was good to talk to your mother this evening and I know that I feel better for it. I only wish that I could talk to my father like that, because I know things would be better at home.

I think we had better get to sleep before we both get into trouble for talking. Good night."

MORE NEW FRIENDS

It wasn't long after breakfast, that Cassie's father came over and he was alone so Cassie was finally able to sit down and have that long talk with him as she had wanted to do for a long time.

She was able to say to her father "*I have a dream* that I would like to try to make come true. I know that it will take a little *money, money, money* and a lot of practice, but I want to be a *dancing queen* in ballroom dancing.

When I'm living at home with mother, I like to go down to the *Tropical Loveland* Ballroom and watch all the dancers practice their routines. *The visitors* are allowed to watch from up in the balcony. I go there that often, that one day they gave me a ticket that was *two for the price of one,* for the next heats of the championship but I knew that mum couldn't afford for us to go, so I threw the ticket away.

When we were in Australia visiting Uncle David, *me and Bobby and Bobby's brother,* Brian, used to go to the dam fishing and one day I told them about my dream.

Bobby asked "*Does your mother know* and does *mamma Mia* know about your dream of wanting to be a *dancing queen?*"

I shook my head "No."

Brian said "You live in your *dream world* because *mamma Mia* won't let you do anything like that. She loves your dad but she loves *money, money, money* more. *The name of the game* with her is; *the winner takes it all* and she will try and stop you from doing what you want and only doing what she wants you to do. Dad has told us that she has been like that since she was a little girl, and he should know what his sister is like."

One day, *mamma Mia* saw me trying to do some of the steps that I had seen the other dancers do and she carried *on and on and on* about me being foolish.

I told her that I wanted to be a *dancing queen;* especially in the waltz, because it's such a graceful dance, and she said "You, you're not graceful enough, so forget your dream, *baby*."

Ever since then, she does all she can to *disillusion* me and I feel like I'm *under attack* from her every time that we are alone together."

Her father said to her "I knew that your *mamma Mia* was trying to stop us talking, but now I know why. Her attitude changes every holiday when we know that you're coming. *Does your mother know* about your dream?"

"No." said Cassie.

"Well." said her father "leave it with me for now and when I take you home after this holiday, I will talk to your mother and she can find out the necessary information and tell me and I will pay for all your needs. I promise you *baby,* that if it's possible, you will become the *dancing queen* that you have dreamed of becoming but you have to promise me, that you will try hard and do the practice needed. When you get to the heats, you have to send me one of those *two for the price of one tickets*.

Now you run along with the others and enjoy the rest of your holiday and don't you let *mamma Mia* stop you from living your dream. I will always find time to talk with you so that you'll never feel like running away again. Okay."

As Cassie ran off to join the other children, who had gone to the playground, she heard her father say to *Chiquitita*'s parents "Thank you for all your help with my daughter. We had thought she had gone to bed early last night; we had no idea that she had intended to run away. *Love isn't easy but it sure is hard enough* to give and make everyone happy, when you're in my position. I am a *man in the middle* when it comes to both my families.

I was one of the *soldiers* in the *Super Trouper* Company that my daughter talked about yesterday but my first wife was unable to handle the army life so we ended up divorced.

I also did three tours of duty but after the last one, I was discharged due to an illness that I picked up in one of the Asian countries. I received a decent payout and I worked as a teacher for a while before I joined CMA, a company like *Intermezzo No. 1* in America. Just like *Intermezzo No. 1* CMA is a corporation that has a lot to do with many varieties of music and it didn't take long for them to appoint me head of the company.

I saved and then invested the little money I had and now I have a lot of *money, money, money* that my second wife likes to spend. I also give my first wife some *money, money, money* to help with the upkeep of Cassie.

I am also working on another project as well. Mia is going to be very annoyed, when she finds out that I am going to put my daughter through

10

dancing school. I always knew that Cassie loved to *dance* but I didn't know that her dream was to become the waltz *dancing queen*. I will do all I can for her because she is *my love, my life* who I cherish dearly.

I intend to go out this afternoon and *bang-a-boomerang* or two if you would like to join me and maybe after that, we could get together and have a good old Australian Bar-be-cue. I know that Cassie would enjoy that."

While Nina was riding her *tiger, Dum Dum Diddle* on the *Merry-Go-Round* and *Hasta Manana* was going *head over heels* down the grassy mound, two more children came to play in the playground. They seemed different and shy, so *Fernando* went over to talk to them.

The young girl said with a strange accent "My name is *Reina Danzante* and he is *Felicidad* and we have just arrived here from *En Karusell*."

Fernando asked *"He is your brother;* isn't he?"

"Si, he is my little brother and are all these others your brothers and sisters? asked Reina.

Felicidad said *"Dame! Dame! Dame! mi hombre pelota de goma (Gimme! Gimme! Gimme!* my *rubber ball man)* Reina, *Dame! Dame! Dame! mi hombre pelota de goma (Gimme! Gimme! Gimme!* my *rubber ball man) Dame! Dame! Dame!* ahora *(Gimme! Gimme! Gimme now)."*

Reina looked at her brother and said "We must speak English when we are out because mama told us that is they only way for us to learn to speak it properly."

Hasta Manana came over and introduced himself and said "Call me Hasta, the only time I get called *Hasta Manana* is either when I'm in trouble or when the others tease me. That's my twin sister, Nina, over there by the Merry-Go-Round. What are your names?"

"My name is *Reina Danzante* and this is *Felicidad,* my brother."

Hasta said to Reina "If *he is your brother,* then how come you look so different?"

Reina said "My papa is a blonde haired American from *happy Hawaii* and my mama is Spanish and has black hair and olive skin. I look like my mama and my brother looks like my papa except he has my mama's dark eyes. Where are you from?"

Chiquitita and Cassie came over and stood beside Hasta and Cassie said "I'm from Australia and I live with my mother in a town north of here, just past the *Waterloo* turnoff. I am on holidays here with my father and *mamma Mia,* my step mother. I don't have any brothers or sisters."

Fernando said "We come over from New York every year to visit with my grandparents in Holland and then we come here to the *Waterloo* Holiday Adventure Park for two weeks before going home. Dad says this could be *our last summer* here but he didn't say why."

Felicidad said "Everyone calls me Felix and I prefer that name." and then he looked towards the direction of the Merry-Go-Round and started laughing before he said "look, there's *Nina, pretty ballerina* dancing over there."

"Hey Felix, come and do some *head over heels* down the grassy slopes with me. It's fun and you feel funny when you get to the bottom and stand up. I usually walk funny and I tease Nina by saying "*I'm a marionette* and I'm going to take you away on my *eagle*." called Hasta as he started running towards the mound.

"Have you been on any other amusements in the park?" asked Reina.

Cassie replied "I have been with dad to the Cotton Bale sheds. It's funny seeing dad trying to *pick a bale of cotton* up and try to build a stack. There is a competition where a person has to *pick a bale of cotton* up one at a time and make a stack out of them. There are twenty bales of cotton and there is a time limit in which they have to make the stack. The person who can stack the most is the winner.

Several years ago, there was *one man, one woman* up against each other and the woman beat the man. It happened to be my *mamma Mia* who was the winner. She was brought up on a sheep station in Australia and during the shearing season, it was part of her job to stack bales of wool. *Mamma Mia* says that to *pick a bale of cotton* up, is the same way as picking up wool, only the cotton is a bit lighter. There are usually heaps more people here on the weekends so they have more competitions on and bands play all day."

Chiquitita said "I was sitting here listening to a *rock 'n' roll* band yesterday and I thought that they were pretty good. I think their name was *Rikky Rock 'N' Roller* and I hope that they're here again this afternoon. What sorts of music do you like, Reina?"

"I like many different styles of music." said Reina "during *our last summer* at home; I was in a school musical *"Hole In Your Soul."* that played to packed houses every night for three weeks. I never had a big part but I did have my own song to sing and three of us girls from the chorus sang *La Reina Del Baile,* which is Spanish for *"Dancing Queen."*

We raised money for the school's music and drama programs but more importantly, we raised a lot of *money, money, money* for a local charity that provides assistance at Christmas time to low income families."

Chiquitita looked at Cassie and said "One day, you are going to be a *la reina del baile* of waltz, so you'll have to *watch out* that you don't hurt yourself while you're playing with us. I think the safest game for you to play here, would be *Ring Ring.*"

Cassie laughed and replied *"Ring Ring* is definitely not my game and it is not the safest for me to play on. I would hurt myself quicker playing *Ring Ring,* than what I would do if I were to *pick a bale of cotton* up.

Where are the boys? *I wonder* if they want to come over with me because dad is getting the boomerangs out this afternoon."

Chiquitita looked around and said *"Fernando* is sitting *on top of old Smokey,* Hasta is doing *head over heels* down the mound and Felix is heading for *Ring Ring.* I can't see Nina anywhere. I'll go and ask them if they know where Nina is and if they want to go with you. I'll be back in a minute."

Reina sat beside Cassie and said *"I have a dream* of becoming a singer but at the moment the *Santa Rosa* Music Institute is not accepting any more pupils until next year. My grandfather used to be a tenor in Italy, when he was younger and he earned a lot of *money, money, money* before retiring. He has told my parents that he will help to pay for my schooling because he has heard me sing many times and is willing to *take a chance on me* being accepted into the Institute next year.

What did Chiquitita mean when she said that one day you'll be a *la reina del baile* of waltz?"

"I have a dream too; I want to do ballroom dancing but I especially like the waltz because it is so elegant and graceful to watch.

When I told *mamma Mia* last year about my dream; she went *on and on and on* about how foolish I was being and how I was just living in a *dream world.*

13

I was telling my dad earlier on this morning about my dream and he is going to talk to my mother about trying to get me into the *Tropical Loveland* Ballroom for training.

Now I'm going over there, because dad and *mamma Mia* are coming down the path with the boomerangs. Do you want to come over and watch us?" said Cassie as she pointed to a large clearing in the park.

Felix went running up to Reina and said "Look, here comes mama (mother), papa (father) and abuelo Vilka (grandfather Vilka). Maybe we can all go over and watch you throwing the boomerangs."

Fernando went over with Hasta to watch Cassie throw the boomerang but today she didn't bang it on the ground first. When he asked her why she wasn't banging it first she replied "These are a different type and I find that if I bang it before I throw it, it keeps *slipping through my fingers* when it comes back." and then Cassie said, "I thought that Nina and Chiquitita were coming to watch. Where are they?"

Hasta said "Nina fell over and grazed her knee and *one of us* had to take her back to the lodge to get it cleaned up. Chiquitita said that she would take her back and tell mom and dad that your parents were down here. She also said that she would bring down some *SOS* drinks for us."

Chiquitita, Nina and their parents arrived at where Cassie and her parents were throwing boomerangs at the same time as Reina's parents and grandfather did. They stood back quietly until all the boomerangs had returned to their respective throwers, then *Fernando's* father, Simon asked Cassie why she didn't bang the boomerang before she threw it.

Cassie replied "These are a different type from the ones we were throwing yesterday and these keep *slipping through my fingers* if I bang them before I throw them. See, even dad isn't banging his."

Reina introduced her mama, Helen, her papa, James and her abuelo (grandfather) Vilka, to the other people in the group that were standing there. Simon, *Fernando's* father introduced his wife Elaine and the children to Reina's family and then Cassie's introduced her parents, Peter and Mia to the rest of the group.

Peter said to Helen, James and Vilka "Later on today, we're going to have a good old Aussie bar-be-cue if you would like to join us."

Vilka said "I may be getting on in years but my memory for faces is still good. Did you ever serve with the *Super Trouper* Company who came to Italy, quite a few years ago and helped us after the earthquake hit many towns? What made me ask was; there was also a man named *Al Andar* who was with the *Super Trouper* Company and he taught a few of the local boys how to throw a boomerang and I do believe that you were with him at the time.

I was with the *Estoy Sonando* Agency and we helped you to *move on* all the young children who were without family members at the time."

Peter stood there thinking for a moment before saying "*Ah Vilka Tider,* yes, I remember you and I do believe that you were singing to the children all the time and getting them to sing with you. It seemed a very good way to keep the children calm at the time. How are you? Have you left or are you still with the *Estoy Sonando* Agency?"

Vilka replied "I don't have much to do with them anymore but my wife still works with them. She has gone to *Scaramouche,* with them and some children this week.

Estoy Sonando has been helping a couple of orphanages to reunite some of the children with their families. Sometimes only an uncle or aunt can be traced; so they are informed of the child or children and are asked if they would like to adopt the child or children and most times they will take the child or children after believing that the family concerned may have perished in a natural disaster.

Some families are split up for different reasons and contact can be lost so the orphanages and the agency try to track the families down so the children can be reunited with them. There is always...how do you say "*Wer im wartesaal der liebe steht?*"

James said "*Another town, another train.*"

"Gracias." said Vilka "I still have trouble with my English at times. I speak German, Italian and Spanish fluently, but not so with English. Now where was I; Oh yes, there is always *another town, another train* for her. In this *crazy world, people need love,* especially the children and the best love of all, is the love of a family. I think that you will all agree with that?"

Elaine said "*Love isn't easy* in some families and due to difficulties in them, the children get neglected and abused so the young ones run away to get away from it. Simon works for *Intermezzo No 1* that has a lot to do with many varieties of music and I do some volunteer work in a very small section of it and I come in contact with a few abused children.

I help teach children to play music on the instruments that we have at our meeting place. *If it wasn't for the nights,* when we have to close, some of the children would stay there permanently.

We have one teenage boy who comes in and sometimes he can be very angry and if we are not careful, he can be destructive; especially to himself. When I see him in his angry state I say to him *"Andante, Andante,* just sit there and play me something, anything and when you've finished, tell me how you feel."

He is an excellent keyboard player and when he's finished playing, he usually says *"I let the music speak* for me. I can let out my frustrations, my anger, my sadness and my happiness through the music. Thank you for being here and *thank you for the music* that helps me so much."

I would like to help him a lot more; however, he is still living at home with his parents. I asked him one day *"Does your mother know* that you can play the keyboard so well?"

He replied "My mother only knows that I exist when she needs me to look after my other siblings while she goes out to the *Summer Night City* Underground Club or when it's time to take the garbage out. *Summer Night City* is one of those places where men and women go for company in the *lovelight* of drugs and booze. At least she doesn't bring her lovers home.

The name of the game that she plays is; you *lay all your love on me* and I will disappear on you once I've had enough. That is why I am so angry at times because sometimes she goes out and forgets to come home for a couple of days.

Enough of my work, I'm on holidays now, so let's go and enjoy this Aussie Bar-be-cue. I have never been to one before."

STRANGE STRANGERS

The following day, all the children met at the playground and this time Felix brought his soccer ball with him. Nina and the older girls found a shady area under some trees and just sat around talking about bands, music and dancing, while the boys played a bit of soccer.

Fernando kicked the ball to Hasta, but it hit a hidden rock and bounced right over his head and some small bushes and rolled very quickly down an embankment that was hidden behind the bushes, so Hasta chased after it. It was quite a few minutes that he was gone and hadn't returned, so *Fernando* went looking for him but couldn't find him, but didn't go past the bushes.

Fernando raced back to the girls and asked if they had seen Hasta return. They said that they hadn't noticed because they were too busy talking.

Chiquitita remarked *"Knowing me, knowing you* and Hasta, it wouldn't surprise me if he was hiding somewhere and laughing whilst watching you searching for him."

Fernando said *"One of us* will have to go back and tell mom and dad that Hasta has wandered off; so I'll go and you wait here just in case he comes back and you girls keep an eye on Felix in case he goes looking for Hasta and his soccer ball. We wouldn't want the two of them to go missing at the same time."

Felix went over to the girls and asked where Hasta and Fernando had gone. "I hope that he hasn't lost my ball because it's the one I got for my last birthday. *I wonder* if one of those two men over there by the trees knows where he is." said Felix.

Nina looked towards the trees and said "What men. I don't see any men over there but I do hear music and it sounds like *the piper* who lives across the road from us back home. When I see *the piper,* I always say *thank you for the music* because it sounds so nice and that makes him smile."

Cassie said "I don't see or hear anything. Both of you stay with us until *Fernando* and his parents get here."

It wasn't long before *Fernando* and his parents arrived, and following a few steps behind was Peter, James and Vilka.

Chiquitita's mother, Helen, sat with the girls and Felix, while the men spread out and went looking for Hasta. Felix told Helen about the two men that he saw standing over by the trees and Nina told her mother about the music she had heard.

The men returned without Hasta but said that they had found a cave hidden by some bushes at the base of the embankment that was also hidden behind some bushes where Hasta had supposedly gone through chasing after the ball.

Peter, Cassie's father said "He's a young boy, so his curiosity might have taken him into the cave. I'm going to get some torches and some rope and we'll go in and have a look around. I don't think that any harm has come to him but just for safety, I'll go and get the things. I'll also bring Mia back with me because she is good at tracking; the Aboriginal tribe near where she grew up, taught her how to do it. I will only be about five minutes. Everything will be alright *so long* as no one panics. Will you guys come and give me a hand to carry some things back please."

When the men and Mia returned, Mia looked around near the bushes and yelled out "*Honey, Honey,* I've found it." and started following some sort of trail that lead down the embankment and towards the cave.

When the men reached the cave's entrance, Vilka said "This brings back memories; it's just like when I helped you and the *Super Trouper* Company back in Italy. At least you know what you are doing. Do you want me to tie one of the ropes to that tree over there?" and then he looked at Simon and said "Don't worry, Hasta will be back with you very shortly and he will be *as good as new.*"

Peter left Simon and Mia outside the cave, while he and Vilka went it cautiously. Ten minutes later, Peter yelled out that he had found the soccer ball and was following the trail of small footprints further into the cave. It took another ten minutes for Peter and Vilka to find Hasta sitting on the ground waiting for them.

As they reached him, he said "I hit my head and hurt it when I fell over and this man came over and touched me on both sides of my head and fixed it, *just like that,* and he clicked his fingers. He told me to just sit here and wait because you would come and get me and take me out safely to my father, so *I've been waiting for you.* Is my dad out there waiting for me?"

"Yes, he is." said Peter "now do you hurt anywhere else and can you walk?"

"Did you find Felix's ball? It rolled into the cave and I came in looking for it and that's when I fell." said Hasta.

Peter said "Come on young man, let's get you out of here and we'll get you checked over properly because you've got a lot of blood on your clothes and face."

Once back at the lodge, Hasta was checked over by a doctor who couldn't find anything wrong with him.

The doctor said "The blood on his clothes is consistent with a bad head wound but I couldn't even find a scratch on him. He may have a bit of concussion but that's all. He did mention that a man in the cave healed his head wound but I have never heard of anything like that happening before. He should rest for a few days, but if he still insists that the man healed him; then I would take him to the hospital for further investigations to his head.

Signs should be posted around the park warning *the visitors* here at *Waterloo* of the dangers of entering the caves."

As the other men started walking back to their own lodges, Vilka turned to Peter and said "Can you remember, the last little boy that we rescued from the town that was completely destroyed by the big earthquake in the hills overlooking Rome. We thought everyone had died because it was six days after the quake that we reached him and remember what he said when we finally got him out "A man came and touched both sides of my head and placed his hands on where I was hurting and healed me. *I've been waiting for you* because he told me that you were coming to get me out and take me to safety."

That boy was covered in blood too, but the medics couldn't find a scratch on him either. You don't think...."

"Vilka, you're right, but people will think that there is something wrong with us, if we go around mentioning stuff like that. *So long* as Hasta doesn't keep talking about it, then everything will be alright. If he does talk about it, people will think that he has a head injury and start doing unnecessary test on him." Peter said.

The following day, Reina was walking back from Cassie's place to her lodge alone when she was approached by two men, and one of them said "Reina, next year you will be accepted into the *Santa Rosa* Music Institute where you will train and become a supreme diva that this *crazy world* will enjoy.

You will even be greater than your great, great grandmother and some of the *money, money, money* that you will make, will go to helping other young children who have a dream like you have. Please tell your abuelo (grandfather) that the last little boy he helped rescue from the earth quake, is doing very well and is now a doctor working with the Italian section of the *Super Trouper* Company."

The men then walked past her and disappeared before she had the chance to turn around and look at them again. Reina ran home and told her parents about the men and gave her grandfather the message that they had given to her, for him.

Vilka asked "What did they look like and didn't you feel scared when they came up to you?"

"No abuelo (grandfather), I wasn't scared at all and I could only look into the eyes of the man who gave me the message. His eyes were blue like the *angeleyes* in my story books. Do you think that he might want to hurt me or my other friends?" said Reina.

Felix said "I told you Reina that I saw two men standing by the trees when Hasta went missing but I didn't really get a good look at them and I didn't tell you that one of them spoke to me. He just said to me that I will be an international soccer player when I grow up and I will get married and have three children but I will always live in Italy. I will think of becoming a soldier for the *Super Trouper* Company but my sport will always come first to me as a profession. I wasn't scared of him either but all I can remember of him was his blue eyes but I wouldn't call them *angeleyes*."

Vilka reassured his granddaughter that both she and her brother were safe and so were their friends.

Cassie was sitting listening to the band *Lovelight* practice when the two men approached her with the sun behind them. As she looked at them all she could see was their wonderful smiles and when one of them spoke to her, he said "Your mother will be delighted because you would like to do ballroom dancing and the *Tropical Loveland* Ballroom will accept you and you will start your training in two months. Not only will you be the youngest waltz *dancing queen,* but you will also be the youngest *dancing queen* in the Jitterbug and in the Tango sections.

Mamma Mia will have a change in her attitude towards you because of your father and a memory of her past. He will be one of the proudest men on earth with what you will achieve.

In years to come, you will start your own ballroom *dance* studio where you will help other young people who have the same dream as you. Please tell your father, that the last little boy he helped rescue from the earth quake in Italy, is doing very well and is now a doctor working with the Italian section of the *Super Trouper* Company."

The sun was so bright that Cassie closed her eyes for just a second and when she opened them, the men were gone. The band had finished practicing so she ran back to her lodge and found her father there on his own; so she told him what had just happened and she also gave him the message that they gave her to give to him.

Her father asked "What did they look like and didn't you feel scared when they came up to you?"

"No dad, I wasn't scared at all and because of the sun being in my eyes, I could only see the beautiful smile of the man who gave me the message. Do you think that he might want to hurt me or my other friends?" said Cassie.

Peter said "I think that you are all safe but we will have to go and tell the others about the two men. It is better to be safe than sorry. We'll go over to see Vilka and his family first because the message you gave me, relates to something that happened years ago when I was with Vilka in Italy. We will also leave a note on the table for Mia, telling her to meet us at Chiquitita's lodge."

Fernando was sitting on top of old Smokey when a man approached him from behind and said "You will not have a lot of *money, money, money* when you get older but you will have a lot of satisfaction from your job and when *people need love,* you will be there to give it to them.

The way that you will give it to them is through the hands on healing that you will be doing. The people will say that you're *like an angel passing through my room* on a dark night. You will choose your profession but you will change your mind when you go to live in *happy Hawaii.*"

When Fernando turned to ask the man who he was, all he saw of him before disappearing into the trees was his long blonde hair.

Nina was on the Merry-Go-Round, not very far away from Fernando when a man came and sat on the other side of the ride and said to her "When you grow up, you will be *Nina, pretty ballerina* and you will dance all over the world.

Remember to always *put on your white sombrero* when you are out in the sun. Tell your parents that I healed your brother in the cave when he fell and badly cut his head."

Chiquitita was sitting reading her book under a tree when she too was approached by a man. He said to her "One day, you will be where your father is today. You will start your music career by doing volunteer work with your mother and then you will get paid work in a different branch of your father's organization.

The organization's president will see that you are always *givin' a little bit more* of yourself to what you are doing and have a natural talent for many varieties of music and dancing, so he will help you to succeed in any of your chosen fields. Your father will not be informed of their decision until they have spoken to you first.

You will be a good influence on a young man named Andante that your mother helps. He is an angry young man at the present but his circumstances will change for the better very soon as he has been noticed for his talent by an influential person, so your mother need not fear for your safety when you are with him.

Tell your parents that I healed your brother in the cave when he fell and badly cut his head. If I had not healed him when I did, he would have died before he was found." She looked up just in time to see his face as he and another man disappeared behind a tall bushy hedge.

All the three children ran back and reached the lodge at the same time and they all started to tell their stories at the same time as well. Hasta and his father came into the kitchen to find out what the commotion was about.

Their mother raised her hand and said "Stop, Stop, one at a time please. Nina you're the youngest so you can go first."

Nina told her family of her encounter with the man and said that he didn't frighten her.

Fernando was the next to tell his story and also said that he didn't hear him approach and he wasn't afraid of the man.

Chiquitita told her story in more detail and told her parents that if the man hadn't healed Hasta when he did, he would have died before help would have reached him.

Their mother asked for a description of the man or men that had spoken to them.

Nina said "He had pretty blue *angel eyes;* like in her story books, a really nice smile and had white hair."

Fernando said "I didn't see his face, only his long blonde colour hair from the back."

Chiquitita said "I briefly saw his face and it was as Nina said; blue *angeleyes,* a cute smile and blonde hair."

Their father was quiet for a moment and then said "I don't think that these men intend to do any of you harm but I think that you should stay near the lodge for a day or two and we should inform the authorities of what has happened."

Simon looked at his wife before he continued saying "I think that we should also tell Helen and James and Peter and Mia. Don't you?"

Elaine replied "*I do, I do, I do, I do, I do.*"

Just as Elaine had finished answering, they heard a knock on the door.

Simon went and answered the door and then called out "*Elaine,* it's James, Vilka, Peter and their children. I'm sending them through to you in the kitchen."

Peter said "Mia is out at the moment but I have left a note for her to meet us here. I expect her to be here in about fifteen minutes."

James said "Helen is right behind me and she will be here any moment. We have come over to warn you about two men who have approached our children today. There is something very similar in each of our children's stories and I am certain that the children are safe; these two men will not harm them."

Simon said "I know, they have approached three of our children and they have just finished telling us their stories and we were about to come over and warn you. What did they say to your children?"

James told them what had been said to their children and Peter told them what he had said to Cassie.

Peter said "When Mia gets here; I will tell you something that makes me certain that they will not harm the children. How is Hasta doing today?"

Elaine said "Both Nina and Chiquitita were given a message for us but Chiquitita's was a little longer. Both were told that one of the men healed Hasta, the extra he gave Chiquitita was because he would have died before help would have arrived.

When Hasta told us and the doctor about the man healing him, we thought he may have had concussion, but now I don't think so. I believe he is telling us the truth, and if he is; who was the man and how did he heal Hasta without leaving any scars or using any medical equipment?"

As Helen was just about to knock she heard "*Hey, hey Helen* what's going on? I found a note saying to come over here immediately."

Helen said "Mia, I think that when we both get inside, you'll understand what's has happened this morning to our children."

Helen and Mia were each given a drink while Simon explained what each of the children had told them.

Peter said "The part of the message that was for Vilka and myself was "Please tell your father/ abuelo (grandfather), that the last little boy he helped rescue from the earthquake in Italy, is doing very well and is now a doctor working with the Italian section of the *Super Trouper* Company."

That little boy that the man mentioned would have been about nine years old at the time and it was six days after the quake that we rescued him. He was covered in blood but there were no wounds on him; he was just like Hasta was when we found him. No one can explain what happened then; just like we can't explain what is happening now, but this time it involves all of our children in what seems to be in a good way."

Mia said "Now each one of you, please correct me if I am wrong about the way the man or men looked when they spoke to you. Reina and Felix, you both saw his blue eyes and Reina; you said they looked like *angel eyes*. Cassie; you just saw his wonderful smile. Fernando; you only saw the back of him, his long blonde hair. Nina you saw his pretty blue *angel eyes,* his really nice smile and his white hair and Chiquitita; you described the man the same as Nina. Hasta did the man say anything to you when he was healing you and did you see him at all?"

Hasta said quietly "He told me that I'm going to be the *man in the middle,* between the people and God and you will *lay all your love on me,* like *the way old friends do*. He said that when I get older, I will know what he means.

24

No, I didn't see him; he was like a shadow because there was a big bright light behind him. When the light went out he was gone. I was like the rest of them; I wasn't scared or frightened of him either."

"Peter, you've never told me that story about the little boy. Now can you or you Vilka, remember if the little boy described the man who healed him before you rescued him?"

Vilka looked at Peter and thought for a moment before saying "I think that all he said was "The man was like a shadow because there was a big bright light behind him. When the light went out he was gone and I wasn't scared of him.""

Mia's face went pale and she slumped back in her chair as she put her hands up to her head.

It was then that Cassie went to her and said "*Mamma Mia,* are you alright? In fact, I saw both the men a little and they both had the same smile."

A moment later Mia replied, "Yes, I'm alright but I had a memory flash of when I was a little girl back in Australia. As you know Peter, an Aboriginal tribe lived close to our station and we often went to visit them.

One afternoon, an elder of the tribe told us a dream time story and now I think that I will tell you all, a part of that story. I don't know if it has anything to do with what the children have experienced today but I will leave it up to you to decide.

Many, many years ago, there was this little boy, who had blue eyes, a nice smile and blonde hair and a little girl, who also had blue eyes, and a nice smile but she had light brown hair, who walked the earth; they were known as earth spirits or angels as we would call them.

Anyway, these two children used to help people who were in danger and sometimes the boy would heal people who were sick or dying. Sometimes both of them would give people messages that they wouldn't understand until they got older or were in some situation that they were able to recognize it.

The little girl was called back to the spirits in the sky but the boy still walked the earth. Sometimes he had a travelling companion who looked like him with him. In our language, the Aboriginal people called the little boy, Earth Angel David.

By the sound of how the children have described the man that they have seen and by what he told them; I would say that each one of them have been visited by this Earth Angel David which is a very good sign. Please don't think that I'm making this up because I have also been visited by this David and today has reminded me of what he told me *so long ago*. I remember a part of what was spoken to me and now I have to correct some mistakes that I have made in the past or there will only be *one of us* leaving *Waterloo* this time." and she looked at Peter and Cassie.

Hasta asked "Mom, what did the man mean when he said that I'm going to be the man in the middle and *lay all your love on me* just like *the way old friends do?"*

"I don't really know darling, but I think that we'll find out once you have grown up a bit more." said his mother.

Mia said "I have a confession to make to my family. Peter, Cassie, I have been sneaking off and practicing for the bale lifting competition on Saturday and I have got my times down considerably since I last entered." and then she turned to the other families and said "I would like you all to come and cheer me on. Being the only female in the competition makes it a bit harder for me to compete.

Now, how about another bar-be-cue this afternoon? I think that after all that's happened so far today and what the children have been told, a bit of fun and relaxation is in order and I'll go and get a couple of boomerangs so we can have a few laughs as well. I'll teach you a few Aboriginal tricks so you won't be saying "It keeps *slipping through my fingers* or for you Vilka, *"se me esta escapando"* when I try to catch it."

Looking mainly at the children gathered around the table Mia said "Now, who would like to throw a boomerang and have a bar-be-cue."

"*I do, I do, I do, I do, I do.*" came the response from all the children except Felix who said "Mama lamentable, no mi *no hay a quien culpar,* se conserva se *me esta escapando.*"

Helen said "Felix, I have told you to speak English when we are not at home, so please say what you just said again, but in English."

Felix looked down and quietly said "Sorry mama. Not me, *when all is said and done,* it keeps slipping through my fingers."

As everyone laughed Mia said "Well, I'm just going to have to take a little more time to teach you how to catch it and keep hold of it, aren't I."

PREPARATION TIME

Hasta was allowed to go and play with Felix on the condition that he was to stay away from the embankment and right out of the cave, so the boys played *Ring Ring* and Hasta became quite good at it. Nina stayed with her mother, to help her with some baking while the older girls were given permission to walk to the main office and shop to buy a couple of items needed for the cooking and the men snuck off somewhere in secret.

As Chiquitita was inside the shop purchasing the items for her mother, Reina and Cassie read the notices on the Notice Board and became very excited because The *Waterloo* Adventure Park were running a few other attraction to the lead up to the competitions to be held on the weekend.

Three activities that caught the girl's eyes to be held in the next couple of days were, supervised bush walking, supervised rock climbing and various dancing exhibitions.

The bands for the weekend were also advertised and they were, *Voulez-Vous, Conociendome, Conociendote, HeJ Gamle Man* but the main *rock 'n' roll band* was *Andante, Andante.*

Reina laughed and pointed to one of the band's name and said "Fancy a band calling themselves "*Conociendome, Conociendote,*" because it's Spanish for *knowing me, knowing you.*"

The competitions were listed and the girls stood there deciding which ones they would like to participate in and which ones they would watch.

Then Cassie read "A combined Italian and Australian *Super Trouper* Company would be conducting the supervised rock climbing and bush walking events."

She was just about to call Reina over to show her the poster, when she saw Reina's mother walking up to the shop. Cassie excitedly ran over to her saying "*Hey, hey Helen,* come quick, come and have a look at this poster. Mr. Tider and my dad would be very interested in it."

Helen went over and looked at the poster and replied "Yes, they would be very interested knowing that their old *Super Trouper* Company would be here for a few days. I don't know where the men have gone but when they hear about this, we won't see much of them at all; in fact *if it wasn't for the nights,* we wouldn't see them at all for the next week. Look at this *dance* competition here; it's for rock and roll and I think that both you and Reina should enter it."

27

"But we don't have partners to be able to enter." replied Cassie.

Helen looked at Cassie and said "Why don't you and Reina do it together and make up your own routine and enter it as a couple. The notice doesn't say that it has to be a boy girl entry. You still have time to work out a routine and practice it. I really think that you both will enjoy it. The notice says that there are several prizes and that *the winner takes it all* so if you win, you can share the prize.

Oh look, here is something for Nina; it's a fancy dress competition. We could dress her up as *Nina, pretty ballerina;* I do believe that I have a couple of things that we could use. Chiquitita is coming now, so you go back to her lodge and I will call over later to talk to Nina and Elaine about dressing her up."

Reina liked the idea of entering the rock and roll competition with Cassie and asked Chiquitita if she could help them to find some music that they could dance to.

Later that afternoon, Helen visited Elaine and they spoke to Nina about the fancy dress competition. "I am sure that I have a few things to make you a costume out of and I think that I know what you would like to be; *Nina pretty ballerina, right.*" said Helen. Nina nodded yes and had a big smile on her face.

Then Helen spotted Cassie walking past the kitchen door and called out to her and as Cassie approached Helen, Helen held out her hand and gave Cassie a small packet and said "These may help you and Reina."

Cassie opened the packet to find four lots of rock and roll music inside. "*Thank you for the music.*" she said excitedly before running off to show the other two girls who were sitting outside in the shade.

Helen turned back to Elaine and said "I hope that you don't expect to see much of Simon in the next few days because he will be with my husband, Peter and Vilka who will be with the *Super Trouper* Company. There is a notice on the notice board stating that they will be here conducting supervised bush walking and rock climbing events on the weekend. They will most probably be here later today to set up the camp and equipment and inspect the intended sites for any safety hazards."

Fernando came in through the back door and said "Mom, I'm bored. I can only climb old Smokey so many times. There's nothing for me to do. I'm bored. I asked Hasta and Felix if they wanted to play a game. I even told Hasta to give me *the name of the game* he wanted to play and

I was expecting him to say *Under Attack* but he said that all he wanted to play was *Ring Ring* and I'm too big to play that. I'm bored. Can I watch *the last video* again before we take them back to the office, please?"

His mother replied "Yes you can, but you won't be bored for much longer. Tomorrow you won't know what you're going to do next, because the Super Trouper Company will be here for a few days conducting supervised bush walking and rock climbing events and I think that you might just be old enough to join in. I will have to talk with your father first, but I think that it would be alright because you will be supervised by trained people."

"Oh cool." said Fernando "I hope dad thinks that I'm old enough and says yes. Where is dad anyway? I haven't seen him all day and he is usually here drinking coffee and eating all of your baking."

"Here." said Elaine and handed Fernando a couple of freshly baked cookies "now off you go and find yourself something to do after you have watched the video and have taken all of them back to the office."

That night around the dinner table of all three families, if the talk wasn't about the coming events and what needed to be done to get prepared for them; it was about the *arrival* of the Super Trouper Company and the events that they would be supervising.

Around the Danzante dinner table, all Vilka could talk about was being able to catch up with some old mates and the young boy that he helped rescue and who was now their doctor. James seemed just as excited about them coming as he wanted to go rock climbing; something he hadn't done since his younger days.

Reina said *"Gracias por la musica* mama (Thank you for the music mother) that you gave us for the competition. There is one good song that we have made a routine for and now all we have to do is practice, practice, practice.

Mama, Papa, (Mother, father); Abuelo (Grandfather) and I have also been working on something. There is a singing competition that I am going to enter so I'm *gonna sing you my lovesong* that Abuelo (grandfather) has taught me."

While she was talking, her grandfather went and fetched his guitar. Reina sang her song and once she had finished it her father said "That was beautiful, darling. Your Abuelo (grandfather) has taught you well and I really do hope that you are accepted into *Santa Rosa*."

29

As her mother brushed a tear from her cheek she said "If you don't win the competition, the person who does will have to be up with the professional singers."

Reina then walked over to her grandfather and gave him a kiss and looked him in the eyes and said *"Gracias por la musica,* Abuelo, (*thank you for the music,* grandfather), and for teaching me that beautiful song. *When I kissed the teacher,* it is because I love him very much. Thank you, again Abuelo (grandfather)."

Helen looked at her father and asked "Isn't that one of the songs that my great grandmother sang and has been handed down through the generations?"

"Si." he replied "Reina sings it very well, even better than my grandmother sang it. The song suits her voice and now if she continues to sing it, it will be handed down to another generation when she is married and has children. Let's hope it doesn't end with her."

Over at Cassie's dining room table, Mia told them that she was very confident about becoming one of the finalists in the bale stacking competition. She also said that she was hoping Al Andar was with the company that was coming, because she would like to have some serious throwing with the boomerangs. I know that *the king has lost his crown* to you but he is also an excellent competitor."

Tonight for the first time, mamma Mia asked Cassie how her day had been and what had she been up to.

Cassie said "Well, we went to the shop for Chiquitita's mother because she was baking and while we were waiting outside for Chiquitita, Reina and I looked at the notice board and saw what was going to be coming up, especially for the weekend.

There are *dance* competitions on and Reina and I are going to enter the rock and roll dance competition on Saturday. Reina's mother has given us several pieces of music to choose from; to make a routine to. I did say *thank you for the music* when she gave it to me. We have made up a really good routine with the help from Chiquitita; she has a really good ear for the beat of the music and can create good moves to go with the beat.

There was also a notice saying that your old company was coming here to do some supervised rock climbing and bush walking activities.

30

Dad, you and the other fathers disappeared early today. I went looking all over for you but I couldn't find you. Did you go looking for the men who spoke to us children?"

Peter was so excited about catching up with old mates and hopefully meeting the rescued young man who was now a doctor.

He said "No, we didn't. Actually, last night Mia came up with an idea and we went to make some enquiries about it and we checked out where the company will be stationed because I saw the notice too. It will be great catching up with them.

Now Cassie, we have a surprise for you. The other fathers and I have been to your mother's place and I have made all the arrangements and have paid for your mother to come here tomorrow and stay in one of the small bungalows beside the office, until Sunday afternoon.

When your holiday with us is over, you will be going home and within the next three months, when there is a vacancy for you, you will be attending Tropical Loveland Ballroom Dance School. I have paid for six months tuition for you and I have set up a special bank account with your mother for all your dancing needs.

Mia told me of the experience that she had had when she was younger and although she can't undo past mistakes, she can certainly try to make up for them. It was her idea to bring your mother here and for the lessons and the bank account. Your mother is in full agreement with these arrangements and will keep us informed of your progress and any dancing shows so that we can attend. Don't forget, I still want those *two for the price of one* tickets and this time we'll be *the visitors,* not you.

I think that your mother will enjoy watching you dancing with Reina and maybe we might even get her to throw a boomerang. Mia and I will make sure that she is included in our activities this weekend, especially with all our new friends that we have made over the past week. Now if you don't have any objections to the plans that have been made for you, come and *lay all your love on me* and Mia."

Getting off her chair quickly and with a big smile Cassie said "I don't have any objections at all. For you to want to *take a chance on me* is awesome; and I promise both of you that I won't let you down.

Mamma Mia, I know that when I'm around, *love isn't easy* for you because we both have to share dad but thank you for your idea of bringing mum up here for a few days.

I am just a girl and *I have a dream* that to start off with, is going to cost a little bit of *money, money, money* but I promise you that I won't waste it on you. I will listen to what I'm told and I will practice and practice.

The man with the nice smile told me that dad will be the proudest man on earth because of my dancing, and you and mum will both be the proudest mothers. I love you both and thank you again."

Now, at the last household's dining room table, there was a lot of chatter going on.

"Anyone want a *SOS,* there is only Orange and Diet Cola left. There is Apple or Blackcurrant juice here as well." yelled Hasta.

As he came back into the room with the ordered drinks, he said "Dad, I have been playing *Ring Ring* all day and it's a cool game. I'm getting pretty good at it and I kept beating Felix. I have worked out how to conquer it and I tried to show Felix how to do it, but I don't think he understood me very well."

Nina said "Dad, on Saturday there is a fancy dress thing and I'm going in it as *Nina, pretty ballerina.* Reina's mom has the stuff to make the costume so mom is going to help her. Do you think that I'll look pretty?"

"Yes." said her father, "you always look pretty to me, and what have you been up to today Chiquitita?"

"Mom let me go to the shop for her with Cassie and Reina and while I was in the shop, the other two girls checked out the notice board for what's on, on the weekend. There is going to be some good bands playing but not the one I have been watching this week.

Cassie and Reina are going to enter the rock and roll competition and Reina's mother gave Cassie some music to choose from. We did say *thank you for the music* but there was this one song, *Rock Me* Tonight that I was able to pick the beat up quite quickly to and the moves seemed so natural to do. Cassie and Reina were also able to pick the beat so together we made a good routine for them to dance. All they have to do now is practice, practice and practice. *So long* as they don't forget the routine, I think that they could win the competition."

Fernando said "I came home because I've been bored nearly all day. There are only so many times that you can climb up Old Smokey and *sitting in the palmtree* gets very uncomfortable after a while.

I asked Hasta if he wanted to give me *the name of the game* that he would have liked to play but instead of the game he usually wants to play he wanted to stay and play *Ring Ring* instead. I couldn't play that with him because I'm too big. I thought that he would have jumped at the chance to play *Under Attack* but no, he wanted to conquer *Ring Ring*. When I came home, mom told me that the girls had told her that Super Trouper Company were going to be here for the next few days doing supervised activities and maybe you might let me do a couple of them."

His father said "I will discuss it with your mother later and I will give you our decision in the morning. Now any one for a game of *Gimme! Gimme! Gimme!* once we've cleaned up?

The children helped their mother clean up after the meal and their father set up the game of *Gimme! Gimme! Gimme!* but there were no chocolates to play for.

As the children sat at their places around the game, their mother said "Now, who likes Marshmallows?"

A unanimous shout of "*I do, I do, I do, I do, I do.*" came from the each of the children and their father.

Their mother then asked "Who like peppermint sticks?"

Again there was a unanimous shout of "*I do, I do, I do, I do, I do.*" from the children and their father.

They were each handed a bag that contained the delectable candy pieces to play with.

Chiquitita said as she looked at Nina "If *the winner takes it all* tonight and eats it all, then we'll all know tomorrow because they will have a big tummy ache."

"Dad." said Fernando "Did you and the other fathers go looking today for the man who spoke to us yesterday? It was very unusual for you not to be here drinking coffee while mom was baking."

"Am I that predictable?" was his father's reply. "No, I didn't go looking for the man. I don't think that we will see him again. Peter had some business to attend to so I went with him. Now, whose turn is it?"

"Fernando, I fixed your torn pants and they look *as good as new* and the next time you go *sitting in the palmtree,* please be careful when you're coming down." said his mother and then she turned to her

33

husband, smiled and said "Yes, my dear, *when all is said and done,* you are predictable at certain times; especially when it comes to my baking."

Nina said "If I am going to take all your candy, then we had better keep playing *Gimme! Gimme! Gimme!* Chiquitita isn't it about time that you give us *the name of the game* that you want to play tomorrow night?"

Fernando replied "Nina, both Chiquitita and I like playing Trivia but I think that it is a bit too hard for you to play. Some of the questions you would not be able to answer; like, *I am the city* where *lovers* often come to and throw coins in my fountain. On the map, my country looks like a boot. What city am I?"

Nina looked at Fernando and asked "Well, what city is it and where is it?"

Fernando replied "*I am the city* of Rome and my country is Italy."

"Oh." said Nina "I think that we should keep playing *Gimme! Gimme! Gimme!* and *Under Attack* because they are both easy for me to play. Trivia reminds me too much of school and I have enough of that when I'm there."

Hasta said "Dad, I have a trivia question for you. If the meaning of the *SOS* drinks that we have here, is Soft On Sugar, then why are they still so sweet and why is there a Diet Cola?"

His father replied "Most drinks have some sort of sugar in them. Some, like fruit juices have a natural sugar in them and others have sugar added to them and being sweet is one reason why people buy them. The company that makes *SOS* is saying that they use less sugar than some other brands and that the Diet Cola has less sugar again.

Drinking them too often is not really good for you, but for special treats like now, while we are on holidays is not that bad. You drink a lot of water that is good for you and fruit juice and your mother and I know what sort of soft drinks are best and we have found that here at *Waterloo,* *SOS* is the best as it does have less sugar in it than some of the other brands. It's also like tonight; we are playing for candy instead of chocolate. When I was out with Peter, I found this store that sells sugar free candy so I bought a few different types and that is what you have been eating."

"This doesn't taste like sugar free candy. It tastes like any other candy that you can buy in the stores." said Nina.

"What other candy do you have hiding daddy?"

Her father looked at her and said "You will have to wait for another night to find out, won't you. Now let's finish this game and get to bed. I bet that everyone will have a very busy day tomorrow."

Fernando said "I hope there are some honey bears hidden away because I like the taste of *honey, honey*. Does any other person here like the taste of *honey, honey?*"

"*I do, I do, I do, I do, I do*." was the reply from all the rest of his family.

REUNIONS

All three families were up and out early. Mia headed for the shed to practice and try to get her time down as she tried to *pick a bale of cotton* up and stack it on top of eight other bales that she had already stacked. Cassie and Peter headed over to Reina's lodge where Cassie would go off with Reina to meet up with Chiquitita and Peter would go off with Vilka to meet with their old mates from the company. Peter had made arrangements to meet Simon on the way so that he and James could go with them for their reunion.

After Helen had finished making some Voul-au-vents, she and Felix finished tiding up before they too headed for Chiquitita's place, where Felix would go and try to conquer *Ring Ring* with Hasta and Helen would help Elaine to make Nina's costume.

Cassie, Reina and Chiquitita took their portable tape recorder down to the Rotunda to practice their routine for the competition but their *arrival* interrupted another couple practicing their dance routine to the *King Kong song, Hole In Your Soul* so the girls went for a short walk to the stage area to listen to *Voulez-Vous* rehearse before *Conociendome, Conociendote* took to the stage for their rehearsal.

Hasta showed Felix again how to conquer the *Ring, Ring* game and this time Felix did it, albeit in a clumsy fashion. It took Felix nearly an hour to conquer *Ring Ring* and the rest of the morning to be able to do it like Hasta could. Before long the boys were racing each other to the top.

A very excited Nina stayed with her mother and Helen whilst they made her ballerina costume for the fancy dress competition.

Helen asked Nina "What are you going to do if *the winner takes it all* and you are the winner?"

Nina replied "I don't know what the prize is, but I think that I would share it with my family and friends if I could. *My mama said* that it would be wrong not to share if I had a lot of different prizes and I didn't want them all or I couldn't use them. If there was chocolate in the prize, I don't think that I would give Hasta some."

"Why not, *he is your brother* and you just told me that you would share with your family and friends." said Helen.

"I know." said Nina "but he would want to eat it all, like he does when he wins *Under Attack*."

The other children returned to Chiquitita's lodge for lunch and an excited Felix told his mother that he could now climb *Ring Ring* just like Hasta could. Felix asked his mother if they could have the *Voulez-Vous* for lunch.

Hasta asked Felix why he called them *Voulez-Vous* and not by their real name, Voul-au-vents, and Felix answered "I couldn't say their right name when I was younger so I called them *Voulez-Vous* and I have been calling them that ever since. Once you taste them, you can call them anything you like because they are so nice. Mamma makes them better than the bought ones."

Elaine, Chiquita's mother asked Cassie to go and see if her mother was back from her practice and if she was, would she like to come and have lunch with them.

As the men approached the Super Trouper camp, Vilka said "I can see Aldo, Al Andar, Victor and Mick but I can't see anyone else we know."

Peter said "Wait a minute; *here comes Rubie Jamie* and Alex."

Vilka said "*What about Livingston,* he was always with those three. I hope nothing has happened to him?"

Alex approached the men and said "What took you so long; *I've been waiting for you* to get here. Come on down to the base camp and meet the others."

Vilka said "*What about Livingston,* he is usually with you. Nothing has happened to him, has it?"

Rubie looked up to the top of the mountain's rock wall and said "*What about Livingston,* he thinks that he's an *eagle* and can fly. *The day before you came* to the headquarters, Livingston was put in charge of the rock climbing group. He has had to find a safe route for the novice climbers and one that is not too high.

Al Andar has been put in charge of the bush walkers and he is flitting around as if he was as *free as a bumble bee* searching for pollen for making his *honey, honey, honey, honey.* Peter, you had better *watch out,* he's been practicing his boomerang throwing and he is out to reclaim the crown."

Peter laughed before replying "You haven't lost your sense of humour, have you? As for Al, *the king has lost his crown* and he is not getting it back from me. In fact, if a competition came up in the near future, I think that I would lose it to Cassie, my daughter. She has a natural way of throwing and catching a boomerang."

Al walked up from behind them saying "Now, *she's my kind of girl.* I don't mind the age of my competition; however, with you and Mia as her parents, how could she not; know how to throw and catch a boomerang."

Al then looked over Peter's shoulder and yelled out "*Suzy-hang-around* the ropes a bit closer or they'll get tangled." He looked back to Peter and continued saying "During *our last summer* exercises, we were called out, *just like that,* to assist in a landslide search and rescue but our normal crew were separated and it was very hard to work with people whom you have never worked with before. I had to be lowered down to some injured people and on the way down *kisses of fire* kept shooting out of some holes in the rubble and for some reason that I can't explain, the rope kept *slipping through my fingers.*

When it was all over, I found out that the people who were doing the top side rope work were taught to leave a bit of slack on the rope instead of keeping it taught and that's why the rope kept *slipping through my fingers.* So when I'm not teaching novice climbers or bush walkers here, I have to assess the other new members of the team and bring them up to scratch so that next time, they will be more safety conscious with what they are doing.

If you had to *take a chance on me* getting you out of a dangerous situation, you would want to know that both of us would be safe. I also have to check out the bush walking tracks for possible dangerous situations and I have found one that would be very unwise to use because an *eagle* or some other large bird has built a nest nearby and would attack anyone who goes near it.

Hey Vilka, has your wife left you yet because of your trips away?"

"No." said Vilka "This trip is a holiday and I'm here with my daughter, her husband and my two grandchildren. My wife still works with the *Estoy Sonando* Agency and is in *Scaramouche* with some children from an orphanage. It has taken nearly two and a half years to find the parents of the children and make the arrangements to return them to their families. She would be here otherwise and she would be going *on and on and on* about the mischief that she thought that we got up to when I was away."

Jamie started to walk away saying "This way boys, there is someone special here that I want you to meet and he is dying to meet you too."

They walked towards the food tent that was next to the medical tent, when suddenly from out of the medical tent came a young tall dark haired man with a small scar on his forehead and a slightly larger one on his left arm.

Jamie said "Imran, I would like you to meet Vilka and Peter, the two main men who rescued you from the rubble where you were trapped."

Imran put out his hand to shake the hands of Vilka and Peter. "Thank you." he said "it is a pleasure to meet you again. If you hadn't come when you did, then I doubt that I would be here today despite what the man who healed me said.

As I was growing up in the orphanage, I was fortunate enough to go to school and because I got good grades, I was accepted into the local high school where I won a scholarship to go to university to study medicine. The orphanage arranged for me to live with some people who lived near the university. I got myself a part time job to pay for my board and save for my future as well as doing my studies. I graduated from university, fourth in my class and sixth in the whole school for that year.

I joined the army and did my internship with them in the army hospital and later I transferred to the Super Trouper Company. It was while I was serving with them that I was caught in a landslide near my home village and walked away with these two scars. Two of my buddies were seriously injured, but because I am a doctor, I was able to stabilize them before more help arrived.

I also learned that our company is not the only ones who do this sort of work. I know that in Australia there is an organization called The First 24 Hrs Foundation and is a registered Not for Profit Non-Government Organization (NGO) founded by Emergency Services and Public Safety Personnel to provide funding and support when responding to the ever increasing numbers of man-made and natural disasters around the world.

They provide funding, in conjunction with governmental and non-governmental agencies associated with Public Safety in order to support the attendance of suitable Disaster Response Teams in circumstances where funding cannot otherwise be guaranteed within the critical time frame following the occurrence of a major disaster, emergency or crisis.

They also do other things like awarding scholarships to Public Safety personnel from both public and private agencies in developing and developed countries, particularly where training budgets and facilities are limited or restricted. These training and research scholarships aim to enhance professional and academic qualifications in the varied disciplines involved in Public Safety.

The Provision of funding for equipment and training of essential Public Safety personnel with particular emphasis on assistance to developing countries allowing them to respond more effectively to disasters, emergencies and other crises and they provide support in order to link emergency, disaster, risk and crisis management Personnel with a common goal of a safer world, under the aegis of the First 24 Hrs Foundation.

The world has always gone through natural and manmade disasters. They also have a 303 Plan which is designed to prompt you into bringing your family together and take a look at your safety in the home and to know what to do if a disaster should happen. Disaster risk reduction is too important to be left to the experts. Risk reduction begins at home, in schools, places of work and worship and throughout our local communities. I wish that we had something like that when I was growing up."

Peter said "Let me introduce you to James, Vilka's son in law and Simon, a friend that we met here at *Waterloo,* a few days ago."

Alex handed the men a drink and said "Yes, life can be a bit of a muddle. Sometimes *I wonder, should I laugh or cry* at the situation that we get involved in and then I realize that what I am going through at the moment is nothing compared to what I have seen some people go through. *So long* as I can keep doing what I'm doing and helping the people who need help, then, *when all is said and done,* I feel as if I have a fortunate life.

Simon do you have a family, and where are you from?"

Simon replied "I'm from New York. I'm married and I have four children, two girls and two boys. My eldest son is interested in both of the activities that you are going to do in the next few days. I'm afraid my younger son will want to come along but he really is too young for the activities. I might even come along myself because they both seem like fun.

What about you James, don't you think that the rock climbing will be a lot of fun?"

"You're not kidding. I'll be the first in line for the rock climbing." said James "I have done a little climbing in *happy Hawaii* before and I know that after a day of climbing you won't have to *rock me* off to sleep that night."

Alex asked "Vilka, how are your daughter and grandchildren. I bet your little Reina has grown into a beautiful young lady now. Is she still singing?"

Vilka replied "My little Reina has grown into a beautiful young lady and she has a beautiful singing voice; in fact, you can hear her sing on Saturday because she is entering in to the singing competition. She is also entering into the dance competition with Peter's daughter Cassie. Simon's daughter, Chiquitita has choreographed a rock and roll routine for them and although I haven't seen it yet, I hear that they are really good. Felix is just the same. He loves his sport, especially soccer. Helen is just as beautiful; just like her mother."

Rubie said "Peter, have you heard about the cotton bale competition? Are you going to enter in it? Ross, one of our cooks has entered and he believes that there will be no competition for him."

Peter looked at the other men and they started laughing when Peter turned to Rubie saying "Not likely; I am not going up against Ross's competition. Tell Ross, not to be too confident because he'll get a run for his money and big surprise as well."

"Oh, so you know someone else who has entered do you? Are you going to tell us who it is?" questioned Rubie.

Peter replied "What! Tell you who one of his competitors is and spoil the fun. *Me and I* and the other fellers here are going to enjoy watching your faces, as your cook gets a run for his money and I maybe *burning my bridges* before I come to them and it's *just a notion* but I think that your cook may lose. I think that it's time to start heading back now but I will come back tomorrow and bring Simon and his eldest son with me so that we can have a go at rock climbing."

Alex said "Aren't you even going to give us a hint to who the competitor is?"

"No, not on your life." said Peter "I'll see you all tomorrow."

After lunch with the other families, Cassie asked her father "What time is mum arriving today?"

41

Her father replied "Don't worry, my little *dancing queen,* your mother is catching the *Midnight Special* from Moscow and should be arriving at the *Waterloo* Train Station in two hours. I will go and meet her and settle her into the bungalow and, if everyone here is in agreement, we will introduce her to everyone over a bar-be-cue later this afternoon. Mia has everything done, so all we will need to do is cook it and enjoy ourselves. Now, I know that the grown-ups are coming but are there any youngsters who want to come?"

There was a unanimous, excited answer of "*I do, I do, I do, I do, I do.*"

James looked at his daughter and said "Reina, while the food is cooking, maybe you can show us the dance routine that you and Cassie have been practicing. It would be a help for you two girls to dance it in front of other people, so you wouldn't be so nervous when it comes to the competition. If you are going to make any mistakes through being nervous, then you can make them in front of us and not strangers or judges."

Reina looked at Cassie who replied "Your dad is right. If *one of us* does make a small mistake it will put the other one off, so a rehearsal in front of other people will be good for us."

James looked at his son and said "Felix, I hear that you have conquered *Ring Ring* so this afternoon, would you like to show me how you did it?"

Felix replied "*Ring Ring* is good. Hasta has shown me how to do it. Can he come too?"

James looked over to Helen and with a smile said "I think *the name of the game* for Felix now is *Ring Ring.* Come on boys, let's go to the playground now and you can show me this new game of yours."

Mia helped clear the lunch dishes from the table and said "Peter, I'm going to make sure that everything is in order for the bar-be-cue and you had better come and start getting ready to meet Janet from *Waterloo* Station. Oh, by the way, is Al still with the company?"

"Yes, he is." said Peter "and one of the cooks, Ross, from the company has entered into the bale competition. He is so confident of winning because he doesn't think that he'll have any competition. I told them that he shouldn't be so confident because there was another competitor that would give him a run for his money but I didn't tell him that it was you. Do you think that you have a chance at beating him?"

Mia said "Before today I would have said no, but I have dropped my time down by two minutes so yes, *I do, I do, I do, I do, I do*. Thanks for the warning. Tomorrow I will practice a bit harder and see if I can knock a few more seconds off my time."

Vilka called Reina over and quietly said "After you have practiced your dance routine, come back to our lodge and we can go through your song for the competition. Maybe you can surprise them and sing it this evening?"

"That's a good idea, abuelo (grandfather). I would feel better if I could sing it to people I know first. In the *Hole In Your Soul* concert, I performed with other children but this time I'm on my own. The other girls are going now, so I'll see you later." said Reina.

Simon told Elaine about the morning's meeting with some of the guys from the company and then turned to Fernando and said "Tomorrow, you and I are going to do some rock climbing with the company but Hasta will have to stay here. I know that *he is your brother* and will go *on and on and on* about wanting to come, but he is too young and too short. *When all is said and done,* I'm sure that he will understand once we have explained it to him."

As the afternoon went on, everyone gathered around the Rotunda near the playground and the bar-be-cues. Janet, Cassie's mother was introduced to everyone and Simon and Peter started cooking the meat whilst Elaine and Mia set out the salads on the three tables set near each other. Chiquitita introduced Reina and Cassie and started their music going for their routine. *Rock Me* Tonight was the piece of music chosen by the girls and their routine went perfectly.

When they had finished their dance, Janet said to Cassie "I didn't know that you could dance so well. *Knowing me knowing you* like I do, I think that you will become the *dancing queen* that you want to be."

Hasta yelled out "Look at us." and he and Felix rolled *head over heels* down the grassy mound and once they had reached the bottom and stood up. Hasta said as he was walking towards them in a funny way "*I'm a marionette* and I am coming to take you to my hideout on an *eagle*."

Nina squealed and ran to hide behind Fernando while everyone else laughed.

Vilka brought out his guitar and said "Reina, has something to say to everyone here."

Reina climbed back up onto the Rotunda and said "Thank you everyone for coming. This year, here at *Waterloo*, has been the best year ever. My family and I have made some new friends that I hope will keep in contact with us. I know that we all have busy lives and sometimes time is the hardest thing to find, but I will try to write to each of you as often as I can. Now I am *gonna sing you my lovesong* that my grandfather has taught me."

After Reina had finished singing, Janet and Mia had tears in their eyes. Chiquitita and Cassie just sat there unable to say anything for a few moments.

Janet said "*Does your mother know* just how good you are. Your voice and that song had me *crying over you*. In this *crazy world, people need love* and you can give it to them, just by singing that song. Where did you find such a beautiful song?"

Reina replied "My grandfather taught me the song. It was a song that my great, great grandmother used to sing. *I have a dream* of becoming a singer and being accepted into the Santa Rosa Music Institute. The man with blue eyes told me that I will be accepted next year. The man also told me some other things as well."

Then Cassie said to her mother "The same man told me that I would be going to the Tropical Loveland Ballroom and I will become a *dancing queen* but in a few different dance styles. Dad told me that he has already paid for six months of lessons and that he has set up a special bank account for you to help pay for the things that I will need. He also said that you are going to keep him informed as to when he can come and see me dance but he wants one of those *two for the price of one* tickets that we will be able to get.

I love you mum and thank you for being there for me and coming here for a few days. I promise that I will not let you, dad or Mia down, I will become the *dancing queen* that you will all be proud of."

Janet asked inquisitively, "This man who spoke to both of you; what did he look like?"

Cassie said "There were actually two men who looked the same but one of them spoke to all of us children when we were by ourselves. Reina and Felix said that he had blue eyes, Fernando only saw his long blonde hair from the back, and Hasta didn't see him but heard him as the man healed him when he was in the cave. I only remember his smile but Chiquitita and Nina can remember all of those things about him.

He was not scary or anything like that and we haven't seen him since. Why do you ask mum?"

Janet looked over her daughter's shoulder towards Peter and said, *"The day before you came* to see me, a man with shoulder length blonde hair, blue *angel eyes* and a wonderful smile visited me. It was his reflection that spoke to me; *I saw it in the mirror* as I was brushing my hair. At the time, I thought that I was seeing things but like you children, he didn't frighten me. He told me that changes for the better were going to happen for us and he did tell me that you would become a world-wide *dancing queen.* Your dedication to the ballroom dancing would allow you to help others and that I would be a very proud mother and help you.

He also said that you, your father and Mia would become closer and thanks to Mia, your dream would come true. I would also get what I want very soon. I really thought that I was imaging things but now I know that when *I saw it in the mirror,* it was the reflection of the man that you all saw, that I saw. Darling, why didn't you tell me about your dream? I might have been able to work something out for you."

Vilka looked across the playground and said *"Here comes Rubie Jamie,* Al, Suzy and Imran. I wonder what they are doing here."

As they approached Al said "We were just looking around the park and we heard this beautiful song being sung by what sounded to be an angel, so we decided to find out who that angel was. When we saw you Vilka, we knew it couldn't be you, even though you have a fine voice, so could it have been the voice of your daughter that we heard?"

"Not my daughter. It was my granddaughter that you heard." replied Vilka proudly "she does have a beautiful voice, doesn't she."

Then Suzy spotted Helen and said *"Hey, Hey Helen,* fancy meeting you here. I think that the last time I saw you, was when I was visiting my parents in *happy Hawaii* and we said *happy New Year* to each other before I had to take the *midnight special* back to camp. *Me and I* had had a few drinks that night and I just made the train. If I remember correctly, I left two *lovers* dancing under the *lovelight* of the moon to that song.... That's it; *Lay All Your Love On Me.* What did you do with that lover of yours way back then?"

"That lover you are referring to; I married him. James and I have been together for ten years now and the singer that you heard is my daughter, Reina. Did you ever find the love of your life?" asked Helen.

"I wonder, *should I laugh or cry* over that question? No, *my love my life* is the army; however, I did meet a kind and gentle man in a *Summer Night City* club but for some reason love keeps *slipping through my fingers,* so I now look forward to a date with *another town, another train* and people to help." replied Suzy.

Mia walked up to Al and said "Ah, the competition has finally arrived. When are you going to come and throw a boomerang with me or are you going to be too busy?"

Al said "Mia, long time, no see, how are you? Tomorrow afternoon, right here if you are not busy. I hear that your step daughter has become pretty good with a boomerang. I also have heard that Ross, our cook is up for some competition in the bales stacking. Do you know who he is?"

"I have no idea who he is. Why? Is Ross afraid of a little bit of stiff competition?" said Mia.

"You might know or heard of Ross, he used to work on the next station, west of your parents back in Australia. He was the Australian junior champion for a while. In fact, wasn't it you who took the title away from him?" said Al.

"Oh! that Ross. Yes I remember him. When the finals came down to *one man, one woman,* he thought that he could beat a woman until he saw that the woman was me and he knew that he couldn't win. I stopped doing real competitions two years after that. I had to *move on* with my life and I left the station for the city life and a female's job that didn't include station work.

We are just about to eat if you and your buddies would like to join us. I'm sure that there's more than enough to go around. Don't forget that I'm an Aussie and we know how to put enough food on for a bar-be-cue, bush style, just like *the way old friends do* back home for the visitors." said Mia.

Janet called Chiquitita over and asked "Cassie tells me that you were the main choreographer for their dance routine. How did you come up with something so professional like that at your age? Have you studied choreography at some time?"

Chiquitita said casually "No, I haven't studied anything like that; *I let the music speak* to me. I listened to it, I picked the beat and the moves then come naturally to me. Once I had an idea of what the music was saying, I was able to relay the moves to Reina and Cassie.

When Reina's mother gave us some music to listen to, I heard *Rock Me Tonight* and the moves just jumped out of my body and I knew that that would be the perfect song for the girls to dance to. The girls were willing to *take a chance on me* to find the right music for them and we did say *thank you for the music* to Reina's mother."

After a few more hours of reminiscing, laughter, games of soccer and a lot of eating and drinking *SOS,* everyone helped to clean up before they headed off to their own lodges and camp.

Al called out to Simon "I think that you and Fernando will enjoy rock climbing tomorrow, so I'll see you in the morning."

Cassie, Peter, Mia and Janet took the bar-b-que things back to their lodge before Cassie and Peter walked Janet back to her bungalow. As they approached the door, Janet said to Cassie "I have had a wonderful day today. I had no idea that you could dance so well and Chiquitita is very talented to be able to help you girls put such a splendid routine together. I think that the other dance competitors here at *Waterloo,* had better be really good or they won't stand a chance of winning.

Peter, do you think that Mia can win in her competition? I heard Al talking about their cook and how he has entered and thinks that he's going to win."

Peter replied "*So long* as Mia can keep her concentration, then she has more than a good chance of winning. What the cook doesn't know is; Mia is his competition and that she has beaten him before, but we are not going to let him know until it is competition time. *When all is said and done, the name of the game* is to try and win and then *the winner takes it all.* Really, *the name of the game* doesn't matter, just as long as you do your best to win honestly.

Tomorrow afternoon, we will be going down to the place where we were today and we are going to throw some boomerangs. Why don't you come down and show Cassie how you throw them. I think that she will be surprised when she sees you doing it."

Cassie looked surprisingly at her mother and said "Mum, I didn't know that you could throw a boomerang?"

Janet replied "Don't forget that I am an Australian too, and I was married to your father for a number of years. I learnt at the Outback *Summer Night City* Camp that I used to go to when I was younger but I never told you because it was something special that you had with your father and Mia.

Now you go and get a good night's rest and I will see you in the morning."

HIDDEN DANGERS

Waterloo Adventure Park woke to the sounds of shouting and sirens.

Simon was the first person from his family to rush outside to find out what was going on. He saw Vilka hurrying towards the Super Trouper Camp with Peter close behind.

Fernando stood by his father's side and said "Everyone seems to be hurrying towards the camp. I wonder what is going on because I see some sort of smoke coming from that direction."

Simon replied "I don't think that that is smoke, I think that it's dust. Here comes Mia, let's see if she knows what has happened."

As Mia approached she said. "Peter has told me to come and ask you not to take Fernando to the camp today. There has been some sort of cave in and landslide at the base of the camp. We aren't sure what has happened or if there are any casualties but Vilka will keep us informed through James.

We have just found out that *the day before you came* here a couple of *the visitors* who were about to leave, went bush walking and were stranded in a crevice near the crest of a hill because they were *under attack* from an *eagle* that had nested in the tree on top of the hill.

It was hours before they were able to get down and back here and they went and spoke to the *Waterloo* Park's management about what happened. Unfortunately, they were Japanese tourists and we not able to speak English very well, so nobody knew about the *eagle* or its nest.

Al Andar encountered another *eagle* on his bush walk, the day they arrived and erected signs warning other people of the danger but the first one, was not reported to them.

A couple of the other visitors, who also arrived *the day before you came,* went rock climbing this morning and encountered the second *eagle* and in their haste to get away from it, slipped on loose rock and caused a landslide, which in turn has made some holes along the path that has revealed some very deep caves.

As Al and some of the boys were investigating these holes, the ground gave way and they have fallen into one of the caves. A second rescue group was formed and as they were beginning to rescue Al and his team, another landslide happened but that's all we know.

I know that there will be an investigation as to why the *Waterloo* Park management has not erected any warning signs around this place. Look what happened to Hasta because there were no warning signs around the park."

Simon turned to Fernando and said "Run over and tell Helen to bring her children over here and then go and find Cassie and her mother and tell them to come over here as well. We are the closest to the camp and it will be easier for James to keep us informed as to what is going on and he won't have to run all over the park. Elaine won't mind them all being here and the children will be safe and they will all be together. They will be able to play some board games and I have some treats hidden for prizes.

I'll go down and let James know of what we are doing and come straight back."

As Fernando took off towards Reina's place to deliver the message, he heard another loud rumble and turned to see another big cloud of dust coming from the camp site. Once he had delivered his first message, he went to look for Cassie and her mother but he met them not far from Reina's place. Fernando delivered his father's message and stayed with Cassie and her mother until he reached his lodge.

Helen had made a pot of tea for them all and had given the children either a can of *SOS* or a fruit juice. Mia helped to make a big pile of sandwiches for when somebody became hungry.

Simon and James returned a short while afterwards covered in dust and James had a few cuts that needed attention. He also had a worried look on his face and Helen knew that something was wrong.

Helen looked at James and said "It's dad, isn't it. Is he hurt badly or...?"

James replied "He's not dead because we heard him calling out. He and Peter were going to help *Suzy-hang-around* the ropes just above a couple of holes when the ground gave way. The rescue teams are trying to work out the best way to tackle the situation so that there won't be any more cave-ins. I would like to get my hands on the plans for this Adventure Park because I think it is built on top of old mines and the reinforcing timber has just rotten away. With the first landslide breaking through the surface, it has started a chain reaction of cave-ins.

Helen; *does your mother know* that Vilka is here with us at Waterloo?"

50

Mia looked at James and said "Peter, what about Peter. Is he alright?"

"I don't know." said James "My back was turned from him as he was helping *Suzy-hang-around* the ropes. I heard him yell out *"watch out."* and when I turned round, all I could see was dust. I wouldn't worry too much over Peter and Vilka because they are both experienced in these types of situations.

Would I be able to get one of those sandwiches, a can of *SOS* and a couple of bottles of water to take back with me? Simon, we could use your help too."

Elaine said questioningly "Why would you want to see the site plans for. Are you a surveyor or something like that?"

"Yes. I was for many years back in Hawaii. I studied for many years and I was able to detect earthquake fault lines and volcano eruptions. I used to get in close to the volcanoes until one *happy New Year,* I met Helen and I gave it all away to be with her. I am not sorry that I did though."

Mia astonishingly said "James Danzante, you're not the….."

"Yep, that's me, I am that James. Now I suppose we had better get back down there and find out if they have made any decisions for the rescue of all those trapped below."

Fernando said "Maybe I can come and help too. I won't get in the way, I promise. I might be able to run messages for you."

James said "I don't think that it would be a good idea because there may already be too many people there as it is. If I let you come, then Hasta will want to come and he will go *on and on and on* to your mother about me not letting him come. I know that *he is your brother* but he is too young to be anywhere near the site."

Simon looked at Fernando and said "I need you here to look after everyone and to make sure that Felix and Hasta don't go anywhere near *Ring Ring* or any part of the playground.

Why don't you and Chiquitita teach the others how to play *Gimme! Gimme! Gimme!* or *Under Attack.* I have given your mother the candies that I had hidden and there are some *honey, honey* bears in the bags. I promise that if we do need you, I'll send for you."

Once their father was out of site, Hasta approached Fernando and told him that he and Felix were going to the playground to play *Ring Ring* and after reaching the top, they were going to go *head over heels* down the grassy slope.

When Fernando told him that he was instructed by their father not to let them go to play *Ring Ring* or go anywhere near the playground, Hasta ran to his mother crying and going *on and on and on* about not being allowed to go away from the lodge.

His mother said "It would not be wise to go near the playground because of what has happened. Your father has given me his hidden stash of candy so that you could play board games instead. You show Felix the games we have and ask him *the name of the game* that he would like to play with you. Once you know which game it is, I will set it up for you and see if I can get the others to play with you. I will tell you that your father had a stash of *honey, honey* bears hidden away and you do like them, don't you?"

The children were just starting to play the game *Gimme! Gimme! Gimme!* when there was a loud knock on the door, so Elaine went and answered it.

One of the *Waterloo* Park's office staff had an urgent message for Helen and had finally tracked her down to Elaine's lodge to give it to her. The message read "Helen, we have heard about the cave-ins here in Scaramouche. We had just finished our business here and were resting up in the *Summer Night City* Hotel when the news came through. My manager has booked us on the *Midnight Special* Express train and we should be there at *Waterloo* in about two hours' time. Once we reach the park, we will meet and your father can fill us in with the details. Mama."

Helen turned to the other women and said "My mama will be here in two hours along with the other team members and she is expecting to get a report from papa. How can I explain to her what is going on, that papa maybe one of the rescuers that is trapped underground?"

Simon came through the door and said "The rescue teams have located five separate teams trapped underground."

He turned to Helen and said "James has asked me to get the work kit that he brought, his heavy jeans, long sleeved yellow shirt and his boots. The cave that we found Hasta in, has given him an idea that could rescue at least three of the trapped teams safely.

As far as we know, there are no serious injuries but Imran; the Super Trouper's doctor is getting his team ready to examine them when they are above ground. Simon thinks that Peter and Vilka are with one of them.

At one stage, a strange smell was located and *kisses of fire* were seen coming from underground; however, that has put itself out. That particular pocket is being monitored and we are lucky that no one is trapped near there. If anymore *kisses of fire* are spotted, then some of the park may have to be evacuated. If that does have to be done, then James said to move everyone over to their lodge.

Helen, *does your mother know* yet about the cave-ins?"

"Yes." said Helen "they heard about it at the *Summer Night City* Hotel. All of her team will be here in Waterloo in a couple of hours. Now let's go and get James's gear so you can get those people out."

"Hey Hasta, *you owe me one* of your *honey, honey* bears. You just lost that round and you know that *the winner takes it all* so pay up." said Nina.

"I don't owe you one. *You owe me one* and this round hasn't finished yet so don't go *on and on and on* about it. I know *the name of the game* is *Gimme! Gimme! Gimme!* but I'm not going to give you one of my *honey, honey* bears until you win it fairly by winning the round and then we all know that *the winner takes it all*." said Hasta.

Chiquitita approached her mother and asked "Mom, can Reina, Cassie and I go out back and practice their routine for the dance competition. I promise that we won't go anywhere else."

Then she looked at Helen and said "*Thank you for the music* again, Mrs. Danzante. I did think of trying to work out a routine for the *King Kong song When I Kissed The Teacher* but I just couldn't get the right beat. Mom, could I also have a couple *SOS* drinks for the other girls and a juice for me please."

"Yes, you girls can go out back but don't wander away. Reina's grandmother will be arriving here soon so I think that it would be nice for Reina to be here to greet her." said Chiquitita's mother.

There was a small shout from the other room and Nina was heard saying, "*One of us* had to win and I have beaten you so now *you owe me one honey, honey* bear. You know that *the winner takes it all* and that's me again and I love *honey, honey* bears."

53

Felix sat down beside his mother and said "(Grandfather) Abuelo Vilka will be alright, won't he. I know that there are sandwiches for lunch but if Abuela Maria (Grandmother) is coming, can't we make some *Voulez-Vous* for her. They might make her feel better."

Helen looked at her son and said "I think that would be a good idea and I think that it's time for you to start calling *Voulez-Vous* by their proper names, Voul-au-vents. When the men get home, they will be hungry and will want more than just sandwiches to eat. Abuela Maria (Grandmother) would enjoy having Voul-au-vents with a cup of tea when she gets here. Felix, what did you think of the game *Gimme! Gimme! Gimme?"*

He looked at his mother and said in Spanish *"No hay a quien culpar, Dame! Dame! Dame!* es aburrido. Prefiero jugar *Ring, Ring. (When all is said and done, Gimme! Gimme! Gimme!* is boring. I would sooner play *Ring, Ring)".*

Mia said "Instead of us sitting here waiting for new updates on what is happening; why don't we do some cooking. I know that I would like to learn how to make Felix's *Voulez-Vous* and Elaine's non-dairy Apple Tea cake. I'm sure that between us we would have all the ingredients. I can make crunchy Anzac biscuits."

Maria, Vilka's wife arrived at the lodge and had just gone inside when Simon came rushing through the door and said "James did it. He has just directed the rescue team through some caves and they have the three trapped teams above ground safely.

Peter and Vilka were not with them but we think that we know where they are. It's just a matter of reaching them and getting them out. The ground up there is very unstable but James has worked out that the main part of the Adventure Park has been built on solid, stable ground so you are all safe here."

Elaine looked towards both Mia and Janet and said "How can both of you be so calm considering that Peter is still missing underground. If it was *my love, my life,* I would be frantic. I know that *love isn't easy* and that both of you have your own kind of relationship with Peter, but how can you handle it so well, even Cassie is taking it in her stride?"

Janet replied *"Knowing me, knowing you,* Mia, and knowing Cassie; being married and living with Peter whilst he was in the army, you get to learn how to handle situations like this. The only trouble with me was when we were married; I was unable to cope constantly with the situation.

People need love and I wanted Peter to be with me all the time, especially after Cassie was born. *One of us* had to give in and let go. I knew Peter loved his army life and I knew that he wouldn't be able to be happy if he gave it up so I gave Peter up. Mia knew about his army life when she married him but through medical reasons, he had to give it up. Cassie is very much like her father."

Mia continued "Peter has always said *"she's my kind of girl."* when he talks of Cassie. His first job when he got out of the army was teaching Australian History but one night *when I kissed the teacher,* he backed away from me. I knew he wasn't happy and we finally sat down and talked about his issues.

He told me *"I have a dream* that I want to start working on. I am going to give up teaching and use my experiences from the army to become a disaster control consultant. Please *take a chance on me* and help me to get started." I was so used to having *money, money, money,* and I knew that if he succeeded quickly enough, there would be so much more for me to spend.

He also worked for a music organization while getting his consultancy operations up and running. During this time, I became pregnant, but our baby son, Kevin, was born prematurely and only lived for a few hours. To help me cope, I through myself into helping Peter bring his dream to reality and we did it after six months. He was happy with how the things were going in his life and I was happy with all the travelling and the *money, money, money,* that he was bringing in.

The only time that I felt like an outsider was when Cassie started spending time with us. I think that she brought back the memory of my little boy that I had lost. I was so wrap up in my own insecurities; that was until I was told about the encounter that the children had had with the stranger, and that brought back a childhood encounter that I had had and it jolted me into thinking and changing my attitude towards Peter, Cassie, Janet and my life in general.

Oh yes; I am worried about Peter and Vilka but I have a feeling that they both will be returning to us by sundown tonight and they will be *as good as new* and making jokes about their encounter today."

Maria said "Working with Vilka and Estoy Sonando Agency has shown me what can happen in this *crazy world* of ours. The cave-ins that have happened have shown me that when *people need love* and comfort, there is usually somebody there for them and usually those people are strangers.

As soon as our agency heard about the cave-ins here, the manager informed the staff at the *Summer Night City* Hotel that we were leaving. They were told that we were needed elsewhere and that there was *another town, another train* to catch immediately. It wasn't until we reached the station that I was informed that Vilka was involved in the rescues but I had no idea that he was one of them to be rescued. I don't know why, but like you Mia, I feel that they will be home tonight and they will be hungry. It's *just a notion* I guess."

Elaine said "Simon and I were discussing before we came here as to whether it would be *our last summer* coming here. We were saying that the children were getting older and there were never other children here to occupy themselves with nor was there much excitement happening. Well this year has been completely different although the excitement that is happening now was not of our expectations."

Simon came rushing through the front door excited but with a strange look on his face and said "Peter, Vilka and two other men have accidentally been found sitting on rocks in a cave. The first words Peter said was "*I've been waiting for you.*" Suzy and Aldo were going to another site when they found an entrance to a hidden cave. Aldo went and reported it and took back a few more men, including James, and Suzy started securing ropes around the site.

Five minutes after they had entered the cave, Aldo and Simon came across a badly burnt out section and some burnt clothing. They thought the worst but kept digging and clearing out the entrance and about seven minutes later came across Peter and the rest of them just sitting there. Do you remember how Hasta was when he was found in the cave; well Peter, Vilka and the other two are exactly the same except parts of their clothing are badly burnt as well as having a lot of blood on them. Imran is checking them over for burns and other injuries and he thinks that the men will be home with us tonight."

It was a few anxious hours before Peter, Vilka, Simon and James walked exhausted through the door. The men looked worse than what they were. Peter told them about their ordeal and how they ended up in the hidden cave. He also told them that if Hasta hadn't got lost, the caves would not have been noticed. An elderly resident of the area told them that they were the caves that the townspeople used to hide in during the war to escape enemy detection. That was why they were well hidden.

The managers of the Adventure Park knew of two of the caves but had no idea that there were so many more situated underground.

They also knew about the *eagle* nests but no-one had ever gone near them. It didn't occur to them to put up warning signs about the hidden dangers in the area."

Vilka said "I remember walking on a dirt track beside Peter and behind Al and Ross, their cook, and they were trying to find out if we knew who Ross's competitor was in the bale stacking competition on Saturday morning, when suddenly the ground gave way. As we fell into the cave, the air was very heavy and hot. I saw a very big bright light and a shadow of something or someone and the next thing I can recall is, sitting on the rocks with the other guys waiting to be rescued.

At one stage, I do think that someone spoke to me but I'm not sure. Imran says that I'm fine and to take it easy for the next few days. He also told me not to go exploring in caves again unless I know where the proper entrance is."

Peter said "I saw the bright light as well and I did hear someone say "Cassie, *she's my kind of girl*. She will be the finest *dancing queen* that the world will ever know and she will always be saying "*Thank you for the music.*" You told your wife once "*I have a dream.*" and she has helped you to make part of it come true; well now is your chance to live your dream and be close to your daughter. Both you and James will start a company and your first job will be sealing off some of the caves and reinforcing some of the others for historical tours. You will both work with the local townsfolk and Mia will be fascinated with the recording of the history of the area. You will also help someone very special to you fulfil her dream in the very near future."

Mia said "Do you think that it was the same person who helped Hasta and spoke to the children a few days ago?"

Peter replied "I don't know. All I really want to do now is have a decent meal, clean up and get some sleep."

Maria turned to Vilka and said "Look what happens when I leave you alone for a week. You meet up with your old mates and you can't even keep yourself out of trouble. Once upon a time, you used to be out helping other people who were in trouble and now you are part of the trouble. Come on, let's get you home and cleaned up."

Vilka said "It wasn't my fault." and started laughing.

Each family left for their lodges and agreed to meet up the following day.

LIFE'S CHANGES

The following morning around the breakfast table, James and Helen continued their discussion from the night before.

James said "I don't want to be *burning my bridges* before I come to them so I will go and talk to the park managers and owners before we say anything to the family. They will need to erect urgent signs today, before *the visitors* start arriving for the weekend festivities. I do believe that the Super Trouper Company will be patrolling the park and will be ready for any incidents that could arise.

Everyone was very lucky yesterday with no serious injuries suffered; however, I think that your papa, Peter and the other two people had a miracle happen to them. The cave that they were found in looked like it had been burnt out with a flash fire. If they had been in there when that happened, they would have been burnt beyond recognition. *Does your mother know* how bad the situation became?"

"No." said Helen "I don't think that she would understand just how bad it was. *Knowing me, knowing you* the way that I do, I don't think that you would tell her either. I know that papa won't say anything because she'll go *on and on and on* about it and she won't allow him to meet with his old mates again."

James then asked "*Does your mother know* that Reina is going to be singing in the competition tomorrow?"

"No, not unless papa has told her and I don't think that he has. After all that happened yesterday, I thought that it would be a wonderful surprise for her. I have told the children not to say anything to her; to keep it as a surprise."

Reina walked into the kitchen and asked "Will (grandfather) Abuelo Vilka be all right. I know that he was shaken up and very tired last night so I said an extra prayer for him before I went to sleep."

Her mother replied "Yes, he'll be *as good as new* by tomorrow especially now, with the arrival of your (grandmother). Abuela You now have both of your (grandparents) Abuelos here to watch you dance and you will surprise your Abuela (grandmother) with your song."

Over at Peter's lodge, Mia was fixing breakfast for them while Cassie went to fetch her mother.

Peter said "The voice that I heard in my head yesterday was right. I told you that *I have a dream* and we have been working on it; however, the idea of working with James to secure the caves and restore the others could be very profitable for everyone concerned. If it takes a year to do a quarter of the work, then next year the park could advertise guided tours of the caves and we could get some of the local people to do the guided tours because they know the history of them first hand.

Would you be willing to *take a chance on me* again and move over here? It would also mean that we could be close to Cassie. Please think hard about it because it will mean a whole change in our lifestyle and you have to be sure that it's something you're willing to do. Is it your dream that I'm supposed to help you fulfil?"

"I will think about it, but at the moment I have a cook to beat again. If Ross thinks that his competition is a man, it will be easier for me train for the heats this afternoon. If I can get into the finals and Ross does too, then we will face off against each other again in the morning. No dear, I don't think that it's my dream you will help to fulfil."

Cassie went rushing into the kitchen and said excitedly "Dad, Mia, I have just found out that there are only six couples dancing in the rock and roll competition and there will be exhibition dancing by the Tropical Loveland Dance Company on this afternoon. Can we go and watch them? Please, please, please."

Her father replied "I have to do a few things this morning and I'll try to make it back in time so that we can all go. If I can't make it, then I'm sure that your mother and Mia will go with you as well as your other friends. Now let's have breakfast so that you can go and practice for tomorrow."

Janet asked "Cassie, what song are you dancing to again? Is it the *King Kong song "When I Kissed The Teacher?"*

"No mum. It's *Rock Me* Tonight, one of the songs that Reina's mother gave us and we all said *thank you for the music*." said Cassie

"Well, *knowing me, knowing you* like I do, I expect that you have your routine down pat but do you think that you can beat the other five couples that have entered?" asked Janet.

"Do I think we can win? Yes, *I do, I do, I do, I do, I do*." said Cassie confidently. "If we don't win, then the couple who does will have danced better than us. It's not who wins or who loses; it's the fun of entering and doing your best that matters."

Simon slept in due to the exhaustion from the previous day and was still a bit shaken when he did finally reach the kitchen for his morning coffee.

He said "I don't know how those people can do this for a living. I know that someone has to do it, but it is such an emotional thing to go through. I keep thinking that Fernando and I could have been half way up the rock face when the rock slide started and who knows what would have happened. A couple of times I have asked myself; "*Why did it have to be me* over there witnessing and helping in this disaster? I wonder how Vilka and Peter coped with the work; especially Vilka because he worked mainly with the displaced children."

Elaine replied tenderly "What happened yesterday does not happen every day and you have never had the training to deal with the situation. You were there and you helped without thinking about it.

I really think that you should talk to Peter and Vilka about how you're feeling now. I would think that all the rescuers would get a debriefing session after something like that. You should know how it feels when our young people at home get a little crazy and start letting their anger out and start smashing things. All *people need love* but for some it's harder to get.

Yesterday was on a bigger scale but to the people you helped, you would have been a special person to each one of them. Peter and Vilka have done many rescues over the years but I wonder how many times that they were the ones who needed rescuing. *Knowing me knowing you,* if they came to talk to you about it, I know that you would listen to them, knowing that it was helping them. Please try and talk to them today because they will understand and will give you answers that will help you settle down.

If you and Fernando had been up on the rock face, maybe nothing would have happened. If it had happened, just think, the children and I could be *crying over you* and Fernando. Now come on, cheer up, you're alright and you still have us around you."

"Dad, Hasta wants some of my *honey, honey* bears that I won from him after playing *Gimme! Gimme! Gimme!* yesterday and he knows that *the winner takes it all* so why should I have to give them back. He doesn't give me back any winnings that he takes off of me when I lose after playing Under Attack." cried Nina as she came running in from the other room with Hasta behind her.

"Hasta, you know the rules to the games. If Nina won, then she gets to keep the winnings. If she wants to share them with you, then it's up to her." said his father and then he turned to his wife and said "you know, when you told me that we were having twins, I didn't realize just how much I would enjoy them being around. I feel lucky because I got *two for the price of one;* in fact, you and the children are *my love, my life* and I don't know what I would do if I didn't have you all."

Elaine laughed and said "*Two for the price of one.* It sounds like we bought them on special from Macys, but I know what you mean. They can be a handful at times but so can Fernando and Chiquitita and you. Some nights when they are asleep, the silence is just *like an angel passing through my room* and I really enjoy it. When you *lay all your love on me,* I know that all the good and bad times are worth it."

"Nina, if you are going outside please *put on your white sombrero* and Hasta, please be careful when going *head over heels* down the grassy slope because there may be some rocks lying around that you could hurt yourself on. Have either of you two seen Fernando or Chiquitita?" asked their father.

Elaine said to her husband "I gave my permission for both of them to go with Cassie to watch her mother compete in the trials for the bale lifting competition. I also think that Janet will be with them. I was thinking of going down to watch her once I've tidied up in here. Do you want to come down too?"

"No. I think that I'll wander over to talk to Vilka like you suggested. I want to find out how he is feeling today." said Simon.

Nina and Hasta returned to the lodge just as their mother was about to leave for the bale lifting trials.

"The playground is closed because it is still too dangerous for us to play there. I really wanted to go *head over heels* down the slope a few times and I think that Nina wanted to ride on the Merry-Go-Round." said a disappointed Hasta.

"How about we go over and get Reina and Felix and then we'll go and watch Mia, lift a few bales of cotton. She has told us about it and I think it may be a bit of fun to watch. We can take a few cans of *SOS* with us and some cookies. Now does anyone know where our small basket is so that I can put the drinks and cookies in?" suggested their mother.

"*I do, I do, I do. I do. I do*." said Hasta running towards the back room.

61

It was fifteen minutes later that Elaine and the twins were walking with Helen, Reina and Felix down towards the bale lifting shed. The children were excited about the following day's activities. Helen and Elaine talked about the effect that the previous day had caused to their respective spouses and families.

Elaine asked "*Does your mother know* about Reina singing tomorrow?"

Helen said "No. we're going to keep it as a surprise. It was her mama and grandmother who used to sing that song when she was a young girl. She met my grandfather when she was performing it in a charity concert one New Year's Eve. That was really a happy New Year for both of them. They both started travelling together and my grandfather always said "*Thank you for the music.*" because if it hadn't been for the music, he and my grandmother would not have met."

As they were nearing their destination, Elaine heard "Mrs. Landers, Mrs. Landers." and she turned to see one of her students from New York.

"*Andante, Andante,* what are you doing here?" she asked.

The young man replied "The day after you left for your holidays, there was big trouble at home and my brother and sisters were put into foster care. I was so angry that I went looking for you and when I reached the music room; I remembered that you were on holidays so I did what you had always told me to do. I started playing the keyboards and was really letting out my anger on it when two men approached me.

One of the men was Mr. Bryans, the music agent. He asked me a few questions and then asked me if I would be interested in joining a group called *Lovelight* because they urgently needed a keyboard player. He said that he was willing to *take a chance on me* learning to play four songs fluently in a week because the group was entered into a national music competition.

You know that *I have a dream* of playing music professionally so I told him that I would be very interested. He asked me how I could play so well and he asked about my family so that he could get permission for me to travel and play with the group.

I was still a little angry and I told him about the trouble at home and that when I was angry and came in here, you would always get me to play you something because *I let the music speak* for me. I think that *if it wasn't for the nights* because you had to close the room, I would have stayed there playing all the time.

He asked me to meet him at the *Summer Night City* Hall; you know the hall two blocks down from the music room, at four o'clock the next day. He asked about my family situation again because he may need their permission for me to travel with the band if I was good enough to join them.

When I arrived, he had a group of other people with him including some welfare officers. Mr. Bryans asked me to play for them on my own and then with the group and the next thing I knew, I was on my way to Chicago for my first gig. We won the American competition and we have just won the World Wide Music Competition. We have been invited to play here tomorrow and then we go back home for a short tour.

I have to say thank you to you because you were willing to *take a chance on me* and let me stay with the music room and *thank you for the music* you made me play, for without both you and the music; I would not have had this opportunity. In these past two weeks my life has completely changed for the better. I have moved in with Mr. Bryans and his family and I'm also close to my other siblings and they are much happier now. Mom is in rehabilitation again but I think that she will lose custody of her children for good this time.

I have to go now because we have to practice. Will you come and watch us play tomorrow. We will be on after *Andante, Andante* and before the dancing competition. Fancy me having the same name as a foreign band. There are two girls entered into the rock and roll competition and I have seen them practicing and they are really good."

"Yes, I will certainly come and listen to you tomorrow." said Elaine.

As they were nearing the shed, the sound of a hooter and a disappointing Ohh was heard coming from the bale shed.

The announcer said "I'm afraid you haven't beaten your last effort so therefore you are eliminated from going further in this competition. This brings us down to the last four entrants. The first two highest scores will face off in the finals tomorrow and the next two will face off for the minor placings. Good luck to you all. Now, the next competitor will be Fred Oslo."

Felix said "Hurry up mama; I want to see if Mia is still in the competition."

They watched the last four competitors compete against each other and then the announcer said "Ladies and Gentlemen, the minor placings will be between Fred and William and the fight for first place will be between Ross and Mia. Yes, that's right there will be *one man, one woman* fighting it out and I have heard that this is not the first time that these two competitors have had to fight it out for first place. The contest will start at nine thirty in the morning so I hope to see you all back here then."

Ross walked up to Mia and said "Now I know why nobody would tell me who my competition was. *Knowing me, knowing you* like I do, I would not have been so confident. I would have put in some extra time and effort to try and beat you. Good luck for tomorrow."

Mia replied "Ross, winning is not *the name of the game;* it's how you play it. I don't know how tomorrow will end. *Me and I* have been practicing for only eight days and I honestly didn't know that I would get this far. I was only going to enter for the fun of it. Tomorrow *the visitors* here may put me off and you could win or you may *pick a bale of cotton* up the wrong way and I may win or it could be a draw. We won't know the outcome until the finals are over tomorrow."

Back at their lodge that evening, Elaine was telling the rest of the family about her speaking with Andante, the angry young man that she had in one of her classes and how he was now in a music group that had just won the World Wide Music Competition and was performing there tomorrow.

Chiquitita said "Mom, remember when that stranger talked to me. Didn't I tell you what he said about Andante, "His circumstances will change for the better very soon as he has been noticed for his talent by an influential person and that you will not be afraid when we spend time together?"

"Yes, you're right. You did tell us that. I don't know how that stranger knew about him or who you children were, but I think that I had better take more notice of what he has told all of you." said her mother.

"I think that we should all have an early night tonight because tomorrow is going to be a very hectic day for all of us and I don't want to see a tired little Nina standing in front of the judges. Now off to bed and don't spend all night talking." said their father.

Once the children had said their final goodnights, Elaine asked Simon if he had a chance to speak with Vilka.

Simon said "Yes, we had a good chat while Maria was doing some cooking for tomorrow.

Vilka told me that it was never easy for him when he was at a rescue site. Sometimes he used to ask himself *"Why did it have to be me* doing this." but then he thought of the victims and what would it be like if he was in their place. Sometime he asked himself *"Should I laugh or cry* or show no emotion in front of the rescued children so he started to sing instead.

The victims were usually in a distressed state because of missing family members. His wife was also a solid rock for him to count on because at the end of a really bad day she would just say to him *"Lay all your love on me* and we will move on to tomorrow together." *Love isn't easy* at the best of times and after a day where you could end up pulling deceased babies and young children out from under the rubble as well as their parents, you appreciate the little things that your own family do and say.

Last night he said he remembered after Reina had sung for her parents, she went up to Vilka and kissed him on the cheek and then she said to him *"When I kissed the teacher* it is because I love him very much." and that was enough to help him come to terms with his state of mind as well as his wife said to him "Tonight you will *lay all your love on me.*" and then jokingly said "you will not go near those old mates again."

He then told me that if I am troubled with memories of what happened, I should speak to a professional person about it and *so long* as I have the love of my family, I will make it through and it will become easier for me. He also said that it may take a few months but he doesn't think that I will have any lasting issues.

I know that he is looking forward to tomorrow because Maria was making some of Felix's *Voulez-Vous* and some of her delicious salads."

Elaine looked at him and said quietly as she took him by the hand "I might just take a leaf out of Maria's book. Come with me and *lay all your love on me* and then we will let the peace and quiet of the evening be *like an angel passing through my room* or should I say our room."

Peter apologized to Mia for not being at the heats that day and told her that he and James had met with the park owners and they had put forward the suggestion of securing the park and making a tourist attraction of the hidden caves. The owners seemed very interested and would consider the idea; however, they would not be making any decisions until after the weekend activities were over. They would erect warning signs about the dangers and fence off certain section of the park to all the visitors that would there on the weekend.

They were also interested in what the Super Trouper Company had done and were going to work out an information and demonstration weekend for all interested parties to learn about their work. James seemed very interested to *take a chance on me* to work with him and he liked the idea of becoming a company.

Helen had discussed with him last night, the idea of moving back over here so that she could be nearer to her family. She was worried that her mother might be away if Vilka was to become ill suddenly and that her mother did not want to give up the travelling part of her work yet. Reina could still attend Santa Rosa and Felix would have a better chance in following his soccer dream.

"I do believe that you will beat Ross tomorrow in the finals and that Cassie will have a marvelous day. I know that I am looking forward to watching the dancers from Tropical Loveland Ballroom. How about you?"

"*I do, I do, I do, I do, I do* think that I will beat Ross and that Cassie will have a marvelous day. Janet will be so proud of her and so will both of us. If our son had lived, I do believe that he would have made us proud of him too.

I have been thinking, that if this idea of becoming a company with James works out and we decide to move over here permanently; would you be willing to consider the idea of maybe adopting one of the children that Maria's organization has helped rescue. I think that Cassie wouldn't mind having a brother or a sister, since she has met her other friends and has seen what it is like to have a sibling." said Mia.

"Why Mia Fletcher, what has bought this sort of thinking on?" questioned Peter.

Mia replied "Since Kevin died, I didn't want any more children and then I found out, that for some reason, I just couldn't become pregnant again. I have watch and have become very good friends to two very different and happy families. I can see the love between them and now I would like a family of my own. Cassie would not be neglected but she would give a brother or sister or both the love that only she would bring them. They could always visit one another and I don't think that Janet would mind either.

I wouldn't have suggested it unless I had thought it through first and I was very sure that I could take on the responsibility of a child or children. Would you please think about it?"

"I certainly will think about it. Having another child or children around would be great. I miss Cassie when she goes home and I look forward to her visiting again. Now let's go and get some sleep, I want you to beat that cook again tomorrow, like you did once before." said Peter.

WINNERS AND LOSERS

Ross looked a bit worried when he arrived at the bale shed. Fred and William were first to compete, with William coming in third, leaving Fred in fourth place. Ross and Mia were next; the final two, to stack the bales. Once the time limit was up for each person, the bales were counted and it looked like a draw; however, one of the judges stated that Ross had made an error whilst lifting one of his bales so that bale was not counted, therefore leaving Mia as the winner and Ross in second place.

Ross walked over to Mia and congratulated her and said "You're right. It doesn't matter what *the name of the game* is; it's how you play it. I know that I had made the mistake but I was hoping that the judges didn't see it and I wasn't going to say anything. I wanted to beat you even if it did mean that I had to cheat to do it and you know what they say; cheaters never win.

I can remember to, when you last beat me. *The day before you came* to that challenge, I thought that I can beat any girl and again with this challenge, I thought that I could beat you easily but being over confident on both occasions was my own undoing. Next time though, I will not be so confident and I will beat you fair and square." and then Ross handed Mia a can of *SOS* Diet Cola.

"The next time, you will win it because I am not going to lift anymore bales. *I have a dream* now that will keep me busy for the rest of my life. If Peter is willing to *take a chance on me,* I'm going to be very busy helping him to make his dreams come true and raising a family.

Now; I think that I'll freshen up and enjoy the rest of the day watching Cassie and Reina dancing and listening to Reina singing. If you guys don't have much on, you should come and hear Reina sing. Vilka has taught her a very special song and she sings it with the voice of an angel." Mia said.

"I'll tell Al and all the other people back at camp who are not rostered on and we will certainly come over for a while. See you soon and thanks for teaching me a lesson that I needed to learn." said Ross.

It was Nina's turn next, to be judged in the fancy dress competition and the judges took a long time to make their decision. The announcer said "And the winner of the fancy dress competition is *Nina, pretty ballerina.* Come up and collect your prize Nina."

"That's me!" said an excited Nina and went up on stage to collect her prize. She had won, one of three board games, a big bag of candy and a family dinner at a local restaurant. The prize judge said to Nina "Just tell me *the name of the game* that you would like to take home and it is yours."

Nina looked at each one and said with a smile "My family always asks me the name of the game that I want to play so I'll have that one please; *Take A Chance On Me.*"

The announcer said "We were going to have a competition for the boys over at the playground but unfortunately we have had to close it down. Would all the boys who have put their names down for *Ring, Ring;* please come to the stage and collect a special prize. Hasta and Felix both went to the stage and collected a book each, a big bag of candy and a family dinner at a local restaurant.

At the stage area, everyone was getting ready to watch the Ballroom dancing exhibition and listen to the bands. Cassie was very excited to see the ballroom dancers in their costumes and they did five different dance routines including the waltz, then she turned to Mia and said "You will all be watching me do this one day."

Finally the announcer said "After we have listened to the next group who has just won the World Wide Music Competition, we will be holding the rock and roll competition so could all the couples please meet over here to the left of the stage. Thank you. Now, without further ado, please welcome *Lovelight* who will sing their winning song, Pass The Love Around."

Elaine watched Andante and remarked on how well his keyboard playing had progressed. After Lovelight had finished playing, each couple in the rock and roll competition took to the stage and danced their routines one at a time.

The judges couldn't agree to an actual winner so they called for a dance off and the music was to the *King Kong song* Angel Face. Chiquitita ran over to the girls and said that the beat to the music was very similar to Rock Me Tonight and instead of doing one particular move once; they should do it twice in a row. It was a difficult move but they had done it a couple of times before by mistake.

To everyone's surprise the moves went smoothly and the girls won the competition which was twenty dollars each and a music store voucher.

Lunch was next and before Maria opened her picnic basket she said to everyone gathered around "I have made a special lunch for everyone to say thank you for what you have done for my husband and me. You have supported us in our hour of need just like we have supported other unfortunate families. We are not as young as we used to be and my daughter and son-in-law can only do so much for us because they have a family of their own.

I have made several flavours of Voul-au-vents or as my Felix would say *Voulez-Vous,* a couple of my special salads and a cold chicken pie. For dessert, I have made a cherry cheesecake. Please come and help yourselves to this lunch and thank you again."

After everyone had, had their fill of the delicious lunch, Vilka turned to Reina and said "Reina, could you come with me please?" He had found out what time Reina was going to sing and he took her with him so she could change and he could get his guitar.

Maria was surprised when she saw both of them on stage after the announcement to start the singing contest was made. Before Reina sang, she looked at her grandfather and said in Spanish first "Gracias Abuelo. *No hay a quien culpar* I *gracias por la musica.*" then she turned to the audience and said "I just said thank you to my grandfather. When all is said and done I *thank you for the music.* Now I am *gonna sing you my lovesong.*"

There was complete silence when she began singing and Maria reached for her handkerchief to dry her eyes. The moment Reina finished her song, she received a standing ovation. The other singers, who followed her, were not received as well as she was.

One of the judges stood in front of the microphone and said "Before I announce the winner; *Waterloo* Adventure Park management and owners have just handed me this message to read. "This will be *our last summer* on this particular site. Next year we are hoping to open a new and exciting Adventure Park. Discussions will be beginning tomorrow to add new features to the park and more activities for the many visitors that we are hoping to entice here. We hope that you will join us next year in the opening of the new stage of the park."

Now, please come forward and collect your prizes when you hear your names. Third place goes to Antonio Frickard, second place goes to Lisa Neringburg and by unanimous agreement; the winner of the singing contest is… Reina Danzante. Reina please come and collect your trophy and your prize. Thank you to everyone who entered."

"That's me, that's me!" exclaimed a very excited Reina and nearly fell over as she rushed to the steps heading up onto the stage. After she had received her trophy and a voucher for her family to spend a *happy New Year* at the new *Summer Night City* Hotel in Paris, Reina hugged her grandfather and said *"Thank you for the music* again and knowing that you could *take a chance on me* to sing the song the way it should be sung."

Reina joined Cassie and Chiquitita and they went up to Helen and said while giving her a small bouquet of flowers and her music pack back "We really appreciate what you did for us and *thank you for the music*. I don't think anyone of us will forget today for a very long time and I hope that we can still be in contact with each other as the years come and go."

Felix yelled out "I have one of the *Voulez-Vous* left over, does anyone want the other one. The last *Voulez-Vous* is going once, going twice, gone into my stomach."

James stood up and said "Well, I have some good news as well. Peter do you really want to make your dream come true? If you can spare an extra couple of weeks over here, the owners of the *Waterloo* Adventure Park want to discuss our ideas with them. They will be paying for us to stay at the *Summer Night City* Motel here in town and to take them of a tour of the disaster site to show and give them our ideas. As you heard earlier, they would like to complete stages one and two by next year. Will you join me or not?"

Peter looked at Mia, then back to Peter and with a big grin said "Of course I will, but are you sure that you want to *take a chance on me* to deliver the ideas that I have in mind."

James's reply was "I'm sure; but are you willing to *take a chance on me?"*

"I am." said Peter and then he said "well let's not sit here too much longer. Let's clean up here, get changed and go out and celebrate. We can use the vouchers that the children have won today if they don't mind."

Nina whispered something in her mother's ear. Her mother nodded yes and Nina walked up to Peter and Mia and handing them her voucher said "Felix, Hasta and I won dinner vouches today. We don't need two because we go home in two days' time. You can have mine, so we can all go out together tonight."

Mia said "Thank you Nina, we would love to go out with you." and then she looked at Simon and Elaine and continued saying "Now, *she's my kind of girl;* generous, thoughtful and kind, just like her parents. My life was a complete mess *the day before you came* here to the park, but I have had an extraordinary holiday this year and it has changed my life completely. I hope that you will come back next year for the opening of the new park and I'm sure that some arrangements can be made so that you can stay as our guests."

Vilka looked at the voucher, smiled and said "Guess where we'll be dining tonight?"

Each adult looked at the voucher and said together "The *Summer Night City* Motel."

Janet said "I'm not surprised. The owners of this Adventure Park also own two more Adventure Parks in Europe and the world wide chain of Summer Night City Hotels and Motels. The day before you came to pick Cassie up for your trip to England, I was offered a job with them. They were willing to *take a chance on me* but I wasn't willing to take a chance on them at the time. Cassie was too young to be left with my mother all week and things were not too good with my mother either. *I have a dream* still but it will have to wait a little longer."

"I didn't know that." said Peter "*Does your mother know* about your job offer or your dream. *Knowing me, knowing you* like I think I do, I would say that she doesn't know. You were willing to *take a chance on me* when we were married and live the army life that you disliked so much, yet you never really said anything. *Does your mother know* about that?"

"No, my mother doesn't know anything about my dream." said Janet.

Mia asked "Will you tell us what your dream is Janet. We may be able to help you, make it come true?"

"*I have a dream* of becoming a Travel Agent. I have done all the studies while Cassie was at school and I am registered, so all I have to do now is to find someone to employ me. Cassie has been my major priority but now she's getting older, I feel confident enough to be able to work part time." replied Janet.

"You are the quiet achiever, aren't you and *knowing me, knowing you,* not really like I used to do, you will achieve everything that you set out to do; no matter how long it takes." said Peter.

72

"*That's me.* Now, who wants to go out and have a nice meal?" asked Janet.

Hands shot up from everywhere and the sound of *I do, I do, I do, I do, I do* was heard by everyone.

That evening, all three families enjoyed their last meal together because the Landers family was heading back to their life in New York, Peter and James had some serious business to deal with, Janet was heading home for a few days rest before Cassie went home and Vilka and Maria were heading home so they could go back to work at the agency.

Cassie and Chiquitita looked out the window at the same time and said together "Look, there's the man who spoke to me standing over there smiling at us."

By the time all the other people looked out the window, he was gone.

The peace and quiet that came over the restaurant for a few moments was *like an angel passing through my room* on a gentle breeze in summer.

That night was the last night that the families saw each other, until they met again the following year and some of the things that the stranger had told them, did come true but for Hasta, the stranger visited him again a couple more times.

Janet's dream came true as she was hired by the Waterloo Adventure Park's owners as their new travel agent for their new park and their other companies.

Everybody has a dream and for some people that dream has come true.

Don't give up on your dream because this stranger might visit you one day and help to make your dream come true.

REFERENCE

THE DEFINITIVE COLLECTION
PEOPLE NEED LOVE
HE IS YOUR BROTHER
RING RING
LOVE ISN'T EASY (BUT IT SURE IS HARD ENOUGH)
WATERLOO
HONEY, HONEY
SO LONG
I DO, I DO, I DO, I DO, I DO
SOS
MAMMA MIA
FERNANDO
DANCING QUEEN
MONEY, MONEY, MONEY
KNOWING ME, KNOWING YOU
THE NAME OF THE GAME
TAKE A CHANCE ON ME
EAGLE
SUMMER NIGHT CITY
CHIQUITITA
DOES YOUR MOTHER KNOW
VOULEZ-VOUS
ANGELEYES
GIMME! GIMME! GIMME! (A MAN AFTER MIDNIGHT)
I HAVE A DREAM
THE WINNER TAKES IT ALL
SUPER TROUPER
ON AND ON AND ON
LAY ALL YOUR LOVE ON ME
ONE OF US
WHEN ALL IS SAID AND DONE
HEAD OVER HEELS
THE VISITORS (CRACKIN' UP)
THE DAY BEFORE YOU CAME
UNDER ATTACK
THANK YOU FOR THE MUSIC
RING RING (1974 REMIX, SINGLE VERSION)
VOULEZ-VOUS (EXTENDED REMIX, 1979 US PROMO)

ORO - GRANDES EXITOS
FERNANDO (SPANISH VERSION)
CHIQUITITA (SPANISH VERSION)
GRACIAS POR LA MUSICA
LA REINA DEL BAILE/ REINA DANZANTE
AL ANDAR
DAME! DAME! DAME!
ESTOY SOÑANDO
MAMMA MIA
HASTA MAÑANA (SPANISH VERSION)
CONOCIÉNDOME, CONOCIÉNDOTE
FELICIDAD
ANDANTE, ANDANTE (SPANISH VERSION)
SE ME ESTÀ ESCAPANDO
NO HAY A QUIEN CULPAR
RING RING (SPANISH VERSION)

MORE ABBA GOLD
SUMMER NIGHT CITY
ANGELEYES
THE DAY BEFORE YOU CAME
EAGLE
I DO, I DO, I DO, I DO, I DO
SO LONG
HONEY, HONEY
THE VISITORS (CRACKIN' UP)
OUR LAST SUMMER
ON AND ON AND ON
RING RING
I WONDER (DEPARTURE)
LOVELIGHT
HEAD OVER HEELS
WHEN I KISSED THE TEACHER
I AM THE CITY
CASSANDRA
UNDER ATTACK
WHEN ALL IS SAID AND DONE
THE WAY OLD FRIENDS DO

ABBA GOLD
DANCING QUEEN
KNOWING ME, KNOWING YOU
TAKE A CHANCE ON ME
MAMMA MIA

LAY ALL YOUR LOVE ON ME
SUPER TROUPER
I HAVE A DREAM
THE WINNER TAKES IT ALL
MONEY, MONEY, MONEY
SOS
CHIQUITITA
FERNANDO
VOULEZ-VOUS
GIMME! GIMME! GIMME! (A MAN AFTER MIDNIGHT)
DOES YOUR MOTHER KNOW
ONE OF US
THE NAME OF THE GAME
THANK YOU FOR THE MUSIC
WATERLOO

ABBA LIVE
DANCING QUEEN
TAKE A CHANCE ON ME
I HAVE A DREAM
DOES YOUR MOTHER KNOW
CHIQUITITA
THANK YOU FOR THE MUSIC
TWO FOR THE PRICE OF ONE
FERNANDO
GIMME! GIMME! GIMME! (A MAN AFTER MIDNIGHT)
SUPER TROUPER
WATERLOO
SUPER TROUPER
MONEY, MONEY, MONEY
ON AND ON AND ON
THE NAME OF THE GAME

THE SINGLES - THE FIRST TEN YEARS
RING RING
WATERLOO
SO LONG
I DO, I DO, I DO, I DO, I DO
SOS
MAMMA MIA
FERNANDO
DANCING QUEEN
MONEY, MONEY, MONEY
KNOWING ME, KNOWING YOU

THE NAME OF THE GAME
TAKE A CHANCE ON ME
SUMMER NIGHT CITY
CHIQUITITA
DOES YOUR MOTHER KNOW
VOULEZ-VOUS
GIMME! GIMME! GIMME! (A MAN AFTER MIDNIGHT)
I HAVE A DREAM
THE WINNER TAKES IT ALL
SUPER TROUPER
ONE OF US
THE DAY BEFORE YOU CAME
UNDER ATTACK

THE VISITORS
THE VISITORS (CRACKIN' UP)
HEAD OVER HEELS
WHEN ALL IS SAID AND DONE
SOLDIERS
I LET THE MUSIC SPEAK
ONE OF US
TWO FOR THE PRICE OF ONE
SLIPPING THROUGH MY FINGERS
LIKE AN ANGEL PASSING THROUGH MY ROOM
UNDER ATTACK
SHOULD I LAUGH OR CRY
CASSANDRA
THE DAY BEFORE YOU CAME

GRACIAS POR LA MUSICAL
GRACIAS POR LA MUSICA
LA REINA DEL BAILE/ REINA DANZANTE
AL ANDAR
DAME! DAME! DAME!
FERNANDO (SPANISH VERSION)
ESTOY SOÑANDO
MAMMA MIA
HASTA MAÑANA (SPANISH VERSION)
CONOCIÉNDOME, CONOCIÉNDOTE
CHIQUITITA (SPANISH VERSION)

SUPER TROUPER
SUPER TROUPER
THE WINNER TAKES IT ALL

ON AND ON AND ON
ANDANTE, ANDANTE
ME AND I
HAPPY NEW YEAR
OUR LAST SUMMER
THE PIPER
LAY ALL YOUR LOVE ON ME
THE WAY OLD FRIENDS DO
ELAINE
PUT ON YOUR WHITE SOMBRERO

VOULEZ-VOUS
AS GOOD AS NEW
VOULEZ-VOUS
I HAVE A DREAM
ANGELEYES
THE KING HAS LOST HIS CROWN
DOES YOUR MOTHER KNOW
IF IT WASN'T FOR THE NIGHTS
CHIQUITITA
LOVERS (LIVE A LITTLE LONGER)
KISSES OF FIRE
GIMME! GIMME! GIMME! (A MAN AFTER MIDNIGHT)
LOVELIGHT
SUMMER NIGHT CITY

GREATEST HITS VOL. II
GIMME! GIMME! GIMME! (A MAN AFTER MIDNIGHT)
KNOWING ME, KNOWING YOU
TAKE A CHANCE ON ME
MONEY, MONEY, MONEY
ROCK ME
EAGLE
ANGELEYES
DANCING QUEEN
DOES YOUR MOTHER KNOW
CHIQUITITA
SUMMER NIGHT CITY
I WONDER (DEPARTURE)
THE NAME OF THE GAME
THANK YOU FOR THE MUSIC

ABBA - THE ALBUM
EAGLE
TAKE A CHANCE ON ME
ONE MAN, ONE WOMAN
THE NAME OF THE GAME
MOVE ON
HOLE IN YOUR SOUL
THANK YOU FOR THE MUSIC
I WONDER (DEPARTURE)
I'M A MARIONETTE
THANK YOU FOR THE MUSIC (DORIS DAY VERSION)

ARRIVAL
WHEN I KISSED THE TEACHER
DANCING QUEEN
MY LOVE, MY LIFE
DUM DUM DIDDLE
KNOWING ME, KNOWING YOU
MONEY, MONEY, MONEY
THAT'S ME
WHY DID IT HAVE TO BE ME
TIGER
ARRIVAL
HAPPY HAWAII
FERNANDO
EAGLE
TAKE A CHANCE ON ME
ONE MAN, ONE WOMAN

ABBA
MAMMA MIA
HEY, HEY HELEN
TROPICAL LOVELAND
SOS
MAN IN THE MIDDLE
BANG-A-BOOMERANG
I DO, I DO, I DO, I DO, I DO
ROCK ME
INTERMEZZO NO.1
I'VE BEEN WAITING FOR YOU
SO LONG
PICK A BALE OF COTTON
ON TOP OF OLD SMOKEY
MIDNIGHT SPECIAL

CRAZY WORLD

GREATEST HITS
SOS
HE IS YOUR BROTHER
RING RING
HASTA MANANA
NINA, PRETTY BALLERINA
HONEY, HONEY
SO LONG
I DO, I DO, I DO, I DO, I DO
PEOPLE NEED LOVE
BANG-A-BOOMERANG
ANOTHER TOWN, ANOTHER TRAIN
MAMMA MIA
DANCE (WHILE THE MUSIC STILL GOES ON)
WATERLOO

WATERLOO
WATERLOO
SITTING IN THE PALMTREE
KING KONG SONG
HASTA MANANA
MY MAMA SAID
DANCE (WHILE THE MUSIC STILL GOES ON)
HONEY, HONEY
WATCH OUT
WHAT ABOUT LIVINGSTONE
GONNA SING YOU MY LOVESONG
SUZY-HANG-AROUND
RING RING (1974 REMIX, SINGLE VERSION)
WATERLOO (SWEDISH VERSION)
HONEY, HONEY (SWEDISH VERSION)

RING RING
RING RING
ANOTHER TOWN, ANOTHER TRAIN
DISILLUSION
PEOPLE NEED LOVE
I SAW IT IN THE MIRROR
NINA, PRETTY BALLERINA
LOVE ISN'T EASY (BUT IT SURE IS HARD ENOUGH)
ME AND BOBBY AND BOBBY'S BROTHER
HE IS YOUR BROTHER

SHE'S MY KIND OF GIRL
I AM JUST A GIRL
ROCK 'N' ROLL BAND
MERRY-GO-ROUND
SANTA ROSA
RING RING (BARA DU SLOG EN SIGNAL)

THE BEST OF ABBA
SIDE 1
WATERLOO (ANDERSON, ANDERSSON, ULVAEUS)
RING RING (ANDERSON, ANDERSSON, CODY, SEDAKA, ULVAEUS)
HONEY, HONEY (ANDERSON, ANDERSSON, ULVAEUS)
MAMMA MIA (ANDERSON, ANDERSSON, ULVAEUS)
PEOPLE NEED LOVE
NINA, PRETTY BALLERINA
SIDE 2
I DO, I DO, I DO, I DO, I DO (ANDERSON, ANDERSSON, ULVAEUS)
SOS (ANDERSON, ANDERSSON, ULVAEUS)
DANCE (WHILE THE MUSIC STILL GOES ON)
BANG-A-BOOMERANG (ANDERSON, ANDERSSON, ULVAEUS)
HASTA MAÑANA (ANDERSON, ANDERSSON, ULVAEUS)
SO LONG

18 HITS
ALL SONGS WRITTEN BY BENNY ANDERSSON AND BJÖRN ULVAEUS UNLESS OTHERWISE NOTED.
THE WINNER TAKES IT ALL
SUPER TROUPER
WATERLOO (BENNY ANDERSSON, STIG ANDERSON, BJÖRN ULVAEUS)
GIMME! GIMME! GIMME! (A MAN AFTER MIDNIGHT)
THE NAME OF THE GAME (BENNY ANDERSSON, STIG ANDERSON, BJÖRN ULVAEUS)
RING RING (BENNY ANDERSSON, STIG ANDERSON, BJÖRN ULVAEUS, NEIL SEDAKA, PHIL CODY)
I DO, I DO, I DO, I DO, I DO (BENNY ANDERSSON, STIG ANDERSON, BJÖRN ULVAEUS)
SOS (BENNY ANDERSSON, STIG ANDERSON, BJÖRN ULVAEUS)
FERNANDO (BENNY ANDERSSON, STIG ANDERSON, BJÖRN ULVAEUS)
HASTA MAÑANA (BENNY ANDERSSON, STIG ANDERSON, BJÖRN ULVAEUS)

MAMMA MIA (BENNY ANDERSSON, STIG ANDERSON,
BJÖRN ULVAEUS)
LAY ALL YOUR LOVE ON ME
THANK YOU FOR THE MUSIC
HAPPY NEW YEAR
HONEY HONEY (SWEDISH VERSION) (BENNY ANDERSSON,
STIG ANDERSON, BJÖRN ULVAEUS)
WATERLOO (FRENCH VERSION) (BENNY ANDERSSON, STIG
ANDERSON, BJÖRN ULVAEUS, TRANSLATION: BOUBLIL)
RING RING (GERMAN VERSION) (BENNY ANDERSSON, STIG
ANDERSON, BJÖRN ULVAEUS, TRANSLATION: LACH)
DAME! DAME! DAME! (SPANISH VERSION OF "GIMME!
GIMME! GIMME!") (BENNY ANDERSSON, BJÖRN ULVAEUS,
TRANSLATION: MCCLUSKEY, MCCLUSKEY)

ABBA LIVE
SIDE A
DANCING QUEEN (ANDERSSON, ANDERSON, ULVAEUS)
TAKE A CHANCE ON ME
I HAVE A DREAM
DOES YOUR MOTHER KNOW
CHIQUITITA
SIDE B
THANK YOU FOR THE MUSIC
TWO FOR THE PRICE OF ONE
FERNANDO (ANDERSSON, ANDERSON, ULVAEUS)
GIMME! GIMME! GIMME! (A MAN AFTER MIDNIGHT)
SUPER TROUPER
WATERLOO
EXTRA TRACKS ON CD
MONEY, MONEY, MONEY
THE NAME OF THE GAME / EAGLE (ANDERSSON, ANDERSON,
ULVAEUS)
ON AND ON AND ON

THANK YOU FOR THE MUSIC (ALBUM)
DISC 1
**ALL SONGS WRITTEN AND COMPOSED BY BENNY
ANDERSSON AND BJÖRN ULVAEUS UNLESS OTHERWISE
NOTED.**
PEOPLE NEED LOVE
ANOTHER TOWN, ANOTHER TRAIN
HE IS YOUR BROTHER
LOVE ISN'T EASY (BUT IT SURE IS HARD ENOUGH)

RING RING (BENNY ANDERSSON, STIG ANDERSON, BJÖRN ULVAEUS, NEIL SEDAKA, PHIL CODY)
WATERLOO (BENNY ANDERSSON, STIG ANDERSON, BJÖRN ULVAEUS)
HASTA MAÑANA (BENNY ANDERSSON, STIG ANDERSON, BJÖRN ULVAEUS)
HONEY, HONEY (BENNY ANDERSSON, STIG ANDERSON, BJÖRN ULVAEUS)
DANCE (WHILE THE MUSIC STILL GOES ON)
SO LONG
I'VE BEEN WAITING FOR YOU (BENNY ANDERSSON, STIG ANDERSON, BJÖRN ULVAEUS)
I DO, I DO, I DO, I DO, I DO (BENNY ANDERSSON, STIG ANDERSON, BJÖRN ULVAEUS)
SOS (BENNY ANDERSSON, STIG ANDERSON, BJÖRN ULVAEUS)
MAMMA MIA (BENNY ANDERSSON, STIG ANDERSON, BJÖRN ULVAEUS)
FERNANDO (BENNY ANDERSSON, STIG ANDERSON, BJÖRN ULVAEUS)
DANCING QUEEN (BENNY ANDERSSON, STIG ANDERSON, BJÖRN ULVAEUS)
THAT'S ME (BENNY ANDERSSON, STIG ANDERSON, BJÖRN ULVAEUS)
WHEN I KISSED THE TEACHER
MONEY, MONEY, MONEY
CRAZY WORLD
MY LOVE, MY LIFE (BENNY ANDERSSON, STIG ANDERSON, BJÖRN ULVAEUS)
DISC 2
ALL SONGS WRITTEN AND COMPOSED BY BENNY ANDERSSON AND BJÖRN ULVAEUS UNLESS OTHERWISE NOTED.
KNOWING ME, KNOWING YOU (BENNY ANDERSSON, STIG ANDERSON, BJÖRN ULVAEUS)
HAPPY HAWAII (BENNY ANDERSSON, STIG ANDERSON, BJÖRN ULVAEUS)
THE NAME OF THE GAME (BENNY ANDERSSON, STIG ANDERSON, BJÖRN ULVAEUS)
I WONDER (DEPARTURE) (BENNY ANDERSSON, STIG ANDERSON, BJÖRN ULVAEUS)
EAGLE (LONG VERSION)
TAKE A CHANCE ON ME
THANK YOU FOR THE MUSIC

SUMMER NIGHT CITY (LONG VERSION)
CHIQUITITA
LOVELIGHT (REMIXED VERSION)
DOES YOUR MOTHER KNOW
VOULEZ-VOUS
ANGEL EYES
GIMME! GIMME! GIMME! (A MAN AFTER MIDNIGHT)
I HAVE A DREAM
DISC 3
**ALL SONGS WRITTEN AND COMPOSED BY BENNY
ANDERSSON AND BJÖRN ULVAEUS.**
THE WINNER TAKES IT ALL
ELAINE
SUPER TROUPER
LAY ALL YOUR LOVE ON ME
ON AND ON AND ON
OUR LAST SUMMER
THE WAY OLD FRIENDS DO (LIVE)
THE VISITORS
ONE OF US
SHOULD I LAUGH OR CRY
HEAD OVER HEELS
WHEN ALL IS SAID AND DONE
LIKE AN ANGEL PASSING THROUGH MY ROOM
THE DAY BEFORE YOU CAME
CASSANDRA
UNDER ATTACK
DISC 4
**ALL SONGS WRITTEN AND COMPOSED BY BENNY
ANDERSSON AND BJÖRN ULVAEUS UNLESS OTHERWISE
NOTED.**
PUT ON YOUR WHITE SOMBRERO
DREAM WORLD
THANK YOU FOR THE MUSIC (DORIS DAY MIX)
HEJ GAMLE MAN!
MERRY-GO-ROUND
SANTA ROSA
SHE'S MY KIND OF GIRL
MEDLEY: PICK A BALE OF COTTON (TRADITIONAL, BENNY
ANDERSSON, BJÖRN ULVAEUS)
YOU OWE ME ONE

ABBA UNDELETED
"SCARAMOUCHE"
"SUMMER NIGHT CITY"
"TAKE A CHANCE ON ME
"BABY" (EARLY VERSION OF ROCK ME)
"JUST A NOTION"
"RIKKY ROCK 'N' ROLLER"
"BURNING MY BRIDGES"
"FERNANDO (FRIDA SWEDISH SOLO VERSION)" (BENNY
ANDERSSON, STIG ANDERSON, BJÖRN ULVAEUS)
"HERE COMES RUBIE JAMIE" (BENNY ANDERSSON, STIG
ANDERSON, BJÖRN ULVAEUS)
"HAMLET III PARTS 1 & 2"
"FREE AS A BUMBLE BEE"
"RUBBER BALL MAN"
"CRYING OVER YOU"
"JUST LIKE THAT" (SAXOPHONE VERSION)
"GIVIN' A LITTLE BIT MORE"
SLIPPING THROUGH MY FINGER
ME AND I (LIVE)
WATERLOO
HONEY, HONEY" (SWEDISH VERSION) (BENNY ANDERSSON,
STIG ANDERSON, BJÖRN ULVAEUS)
RING RING (SWEDISH/SPANISH/GERMAN VERSION) (BENNY
ANDERSSON, STIG ANDERSON, BJÖRN ULVAEUS)

THE COMPLETE STUDIO RECORDINGS (ABBA ALBUM)
CD 1
RING RING (1973)
RING RING
ANOTHER TOWN, ANOTHER TRAIN
DISILLUSION
PEOPLE NEED LOVE
I SAW IT IN THE MIRROR
NINA, PRETTY BALLERINA
LOVE ISN'T EASY (BUT IT SURE IS HARD ENOUGH)
ME AND BOBBY AND BOBBY'S BROTHER
HE IS YOUR BROTHER
SHE'S MY KIND OF GIRL
I AM JUST A GIRL
ROCK'N ROLL BAND
BONUS TRACKS
RING RING (BARA DU SLOG EN SIGNAL)
(SWEDISH VERSION)

ÅH, VILKA TIDER
MERRY-GO-ROUND
SANTA ROSA
RING RING (SPANISH VERSION)
WER IM WARTESAAL DER LIEBE STEHT (GERMAN VERSION
OF "ANOTHER TOWN, ANOTHER TRAIN")
RING RING (GERMAN VERSION)
CD 2
WATERLOO (1974)
WATERLOO
SITTING IN THE PALMTREE
KING KONG SONG
HASTA MAÑANA
MY MAMA SAID
DANCE (WHILE THE MUSIC STILL GOES ON)
HONEY, HONEY
WATCH OUT
WHAT ABOUT LIVINGSTONE?
GONNA SING YOU MY LOVESONG
SUZY-HANG-AROUND
BONUS TRACKS
RING RING (US REMIX 1974)
WATERLOO (SWEDISH VERSION)
HONEY, HONEY (SWEDISH VERSION)
WATERLOO (GERMAN VERSION)
HASTA MAÑANA (SPANISH VERSION)
RING RING (UK REMIX 1974)
WATERLOO (FRENCH VERSION)
CD 3
ABBA (1975)
MAMMA MIA
HEY, HEY HELEN
TROPICAL LOVELAND
SOS
MAN IN THE MIDDLE
BANG-A-BOOMERANG
I DO, I DO, I DO, I DO, I DO
ROCK ME
INTERMEZZO NO. 1
I'VE BEEN WAITING FOR YOU
SO LONG
BONUS TRACKS
CRAZY WORLD

MEDLEY: PICK A BALE OF COTTON –ON TOP OF OLD SMOKEY
– MIDNIGHT SPECIAL (1978 REMIX)
MAMMA MIA (SPANISH VERSION)
CD 4
ARRIVAL (1976)
WHEN I KISSED THE TEACHER
DANCING QUEEN
MY LOVE, MY LIFE
DUM DUM DIDDLE
KNOWING ME, KNOWING YOU
MONEY, MONEY, MONEY
THAT'S ME
WHY DID IT HAVE TO BE ME?
TIGER
ARRIVAL
BONUS TRACKS
FERNANDO
HAPPY HAWAII (EARLY VERSION OF "WHY DID IT HAVE TO
BE ME?")
LA REINA DEL BAILE (SPANISH VERSION OF "DANCING
QUEEN")
CONOCIÉNDOME, CONOCIÉNDOTE (SPANISH VERSION OF
"KNOWING ME, KNOWING YOU")
FERNANDO (SPANISH VERSION)
CD 5
THE ALBUM (1977)
EAGLE
TAKE A CHANCE ON ME
ONE MAN, ONE WOMAN
THE NAME OF THE GAME
MOVE ON
HOLE IN YOUR SOUL
**THE GIRL WITH THE GOLDEN HAIR – 3 SCENES FROM A
MINI-MUSICAL**
THANK YOU FOR THE MUSIC
I WONDER (DEPARTURE)
I'M A MARIONETTE
BONUS TRACKS
AL ANDAR (SPANISH VERSION OF "MOVE ON")
GRACIAS POR LA MÚSICA (SPANISH VERSION OF "THANK
YOU FOR THE MUSIC")
CD 6
VOULEZ-VOUS (1979)

AS GOOD AS NEW
VOULEZ-VOUS
I HAVE A DREAM
ANGELEYES
THE KING HAS LOST HIS CROWN
DOES YOUR MOTHER KNOW
IF IT WASN'T FOR THE NIGHTS
CHIQUITITA
LOVERS (LIVE A LITTLE LONGER)
KISSES OF FIRE
BONUS TRACKS
SUMMER NIGHT CITY
LOVELIGHT
GIMME! GIMME! GIMME! (A MAN AFTER MIDNIGHT)
ESTOY SOÑANDO (SPANISH VERSION OF "I HAVE A DREAM")
CHIQUITITA (SPANISH VERSION)
DAME! DAME! DAME! (SPANISH VERSION OF
"GIMME! GIMME! GIMME! (A MAN AFTER MIDNIGHT)")
CD 7
SUPER TROUPER (1980)
SUPER TROUPER
THE WINNER TAKES IT ALL
ON AND ON AND ON
ANDANTE, ANDANTE
ME AND I
HAPPY NEW YEAR
OUR LAST SUMMER
THE PIPER
LAY ALL YOUR LOVE ON ME
THE WAY OLD FRIENDS DO
BONUS TRACKS
ELAINE
ANDANTE, ANDANTE (SPANISH VERSION)
FELICIDAD (SPANISH VERSION OF "HAPPY NEW YEAR")
CD 8
THE VISITORS (1981)
THE VISITORS
HEAD OVER HEELS
WHEN ALL IS SAID AND DONE
SOLDIERS
I LET THE MUSIC SPEAK
ONE OF US
TWO FOR THE PRICE OF ONE

SLIPPING THROUGH MY FINGERS
LIKE AN ANGEL PASSING THROUGH MY ROOM
BONUS TRACKS
SHOULD I LAUGH OR CRY?
NO HAY A QUIEN CULPAR (SPANISH VERSION OF "WHEN ALL
IS SAID AND DONE")
SE ME ESTÁ ESCAPANDO (SPANISH VERSION OF "SLIPPING
THROUGH MY FINGERS")
THE DAY BEFORE YOU CAME
CASSANDRA
UNDER ATTACK
YOU OWE ME ONE
CD 9
RARITIES
WATERLOO" (ALTERNATE MIX)
MEDLEY: PICK A BALE OF COTTON/ON TOP OF OLD
SMOKEY/MIDNIGHT SPECIAL" (ORIGINAL 1975 MIX)
THANK YOU FOR THE MUSIC" (DORIS DAY VERSION)
SUMMER NIGHT CITY" (FULL LENGTH VERSION)
LOVELIGHT" (ALTERNATE MIX)
DREAM WORLD
VOULEZ-VOUS" (EXTENDED REMIX)
ON AND ON AND ON" (FULL LENGTH VERSION)
PUT ON YOUR WHITE SOMBRERO
I AM THE CITY

ABBA UNDELETED
"SCARAMOUCHE"
"SUMMER NIGHT CITY"
"TAKE A CHANCE ON ME"
"BABY"
"JUST A NOTION"
"RIKKY ROCK 'N' ROLLER"
"BURNING MY BRIDGES"
"FERNANDO"
"HERE COMES RUBIE JAMIE"
"HAMLET III PARTS 1 & 2"
"FREE AS A BUMBLE BEE"
"RUBBER BALL MAN"
"CRYING OVER YOU"
"JUST LIKE THAT"
"GIVIN' A LITTLE BIT MORE"

DVD 1
THE VIDEOS
RING RING
WATERLOO
MAMMA MIA
SOS
BANG-A-BOOMERANG
I DO, I DO, I DO, I DO, I DO
FERNANDO
DANCING QUEEN
MONEY, MONEY, MONEY
KNOWING ME, KNOWING YOU
THAT'S ME
THE NAME OF THE GAME
TAKE A CHANCE ON ME
EAGLE
ONE MAN, ONE WOMAN
THANK YOU FOR THE MUSIC
SUMMER NIGHT CITY
CHIQUITITA
DOES YOUR MOTHER KNOW
VOULEZ-VOUS
GIMME! GIMME! GIMME! (A MAN AFTER MIDNIGHT)
I HAVE A DREAM
SUPER TROUPER
THE WINNER TAKES IT ALL
ON AND ON AND ON
HAPPY NEW YEAR
LAY ALL YOUR LOVE ON ME
HEAD OVER HEELS
WHEN ALL IS SAID AND DONE
ONE OF US
THE DAY BEFORE YOU CAME
UNDER ATTACK
BONUS VIDEOS
ESTOY SOÑANDO
FELICIDAD
NO HAY A QUIEN CULPAR
DANCING QUEEN" (1992 VERSION)
THE LAST VIDEO
DVD 2
THE HISTORY (Not used in story)

DOCUMENTARY (ORIGINALLY APPEARED ON ABBA GOLD
DVD)

LIVE IN APRIL 1981
SELECTIONS FROM ABBA'S FINAL LIVE CONCERT,
ORIGINALLY BROADCAST AS PART OF THE TELEVISION
SPECIAL DICK CAVETT MEETS ABBA.
GIMME! GIMME! GIMME! (A MAN AFTER MIDNIGHT)
SUPER TROUPER
TWO FOR THE PRICE OF ONE
SLIPPING THROUGH MY FINGERS
ON AND ON AND ON

THE ALBUMS
CD 1
RING RING (1973)
RING RING
ANOTHER TOWN, ANOTHER TRAIN
DISILLUSION
PEOPLE NEED LOVE
I SAW IT IN THE MIRROR
NINA, PRETTY BALLERINA
LOVE ISN'T EASY (BUT IT SURE IS HARD ENOUGH)
ME AND BOBBY AND BOBBY'S BROTHER
HE IS YOUR BROTHER
SHE'S MY KIND OF GIRL
I AM JUST A GIRL
ROCK'N ROLL BAND
CD 2
WATERLOO (1974)
WATERLOO
SITTING IN THE PALMTREE
KING KONG SONG
HASTA MAÑANA
MY MAMA SAID
DANCE (WHILE THE MUSIC STILL GOES ON)
HONEY, HONEY
WATCH OUT
WHAT ABOUT LIVINGSTONE?
GONNA SING YOU MY LOVESONG
SUZY-HANG-AROUND
CD 3
ABBA (1975)
MAMMA MIA

HEY, HEY HELEN
TROPICAL LOVELAND
SOS
MAN IN THE MIDDLE
BANG-A-BOOMERANG
I DO, I DO, I DO, I DO, I DO
ROCK ME
INTERMEZZO NO. 1
I'VE BEEN WAITING FOR YOU
SO LONG
CD 4
ARRIVAL (1976)
WHEN I KISSED THE TEACHER
DANCING QUEEN
MY LOVE, MY LIFE
DUM DUM DIDDLE
KNOWING ME, KNOWING YOU
MONEY, MONEY, MONEY
THAT'S ME
WHY DID IT HAVE TO BE ME?
TIGER
ARRIVAL
CD 5
ABBA–THE ALBUM (1977)
EAGLE
TAKE A CHANCE ON ME
ONE MAN, ONE WOMAN
THE NAME OF THE GAME
MOVE ON
HOLE IN YOUR SOUL
THE GIRL WITH THE GOLDEN HAIR – 3 SCENES FROM A MINI-MUSICAL
THANK YOU FOR THE MUSIC
I WONDER (DEPARTURE)
I'M A MARIONETTE
CD 6
VOULEZ-VOUS (1979)
AS GOOD AS NEW
VOULEZ-VOUS
I HAVE A DREAM
ANGEL EYES
THE KING HAS LOST HIS CROWN
DOES YOUR MOTHER KNOW

IF IT WASN'T FOR THE NIGHTS
CHIQUITITA
LOVERS (LIVE A LITTLE LONGER)
KISSES OF FIRE
CD 7
SUPER TROUPER (1980)
SUPER TROUPER
THE WINNER TAKES IT ALL
ON AND ON AND ON
ANDANTE, ANDANTE
ME AND I
HAPPY NEW YEAR
OUR LAST SUMMER
THE PIPER
LAY ALL YOUR LOVE ON ME
THE WAY OLD FRIENDS DO
CD 8
THE VISITORS (1981)
THE VISITORS
HEAD OVER HEELS
WHEN ALL IS SAID AND DONE
SOLDIERS
I LET THE MUSIC SPEAK
ONE OF US
TWO FOR THE PRICE OF ONE
SLIPPING THROUGH MY FINGERS
LIKE AN ANGEL PASSING THROUGH MY ROOM
CD 9
BONUS TRACKS
MERRY-GO-ROUND
SANTA ROSA
RING, RING (BARA DU SLOG EN SIGNAL)
WATERLOO (SWEDISH VERSION)
FERNANDO
CRAZY WORLD
HAPPY HAWAII
SUMMER NIGHT CITY
MEDLEY: PICK A BALE OF COTTON/ON TOP OF OLD
SMOKEY/MIDNIGHT SPECIAL
LOVELIGHT
GIMME! GIMME! GIMME! (A MAN AFTER MIDNIGHT)
ELAINE
SHOULD I LAUGH OR CRY

YOU OWE ME ONE
CASSANDRA
UNDER ATTACK
THE DAY BEFORE YOU CAME

SINGLES
PEOPLE NEED LOVE
HE IS YOUR BROTHER
RING RING
LOVE ISN'T EASY (BUT IT SURE IS HARD ENOUGH)
WATERLOO
HONEY, HONEY
HASTA MAÑANA
SO LONG
I DO, I DO, I DO, I DO, I DO
SOS
MAMMA MIA
FERNANDO
DANCING QUEEN
MONEY, MONEY, MONEY
KNOWING ME, KNOWING YOU
THE NAME OF THE GAME
TAKE A CHANCE ON ME
EAGLE
SUMMER NIGHT CITY
CHIQUITITA
DOES YOUR MOTHER KNOW
VOULEZ-VOUS
ANGELEYES
GIMME! GIMME! GIMME! (A MAN AFTER MIDNIGHT)
I HAVE A DREAM
THE WINNER TAKES IT ALL
ON AND ON AND ON
SUPER TROUPER
LAY ALL YOUR LOVE ON ME
ONE OF US
WHEN ALL IS SAID AND DONE
HEAD OVER HEELS
THE VISITORS
THE DAY BEFORE YOU CAME
UNDER ATTACK
THANK YOU FOR THE MUSIC

OTHER SONGS
SHE'S MY KIND OF GIRL
EN KARUSELL
ANOTHER TOWN, ANOTHER TRAIN
NINA, PRETTY BALLERINA
ROCK'N ROLL BAND
KING KONG SONG
BANG-A-BOOMERANG
ROCK ME
I'VE BEEN WAITING FOR YOU
MY LOVE, MY LIFE
THAT'S ME
ARRIVAL
AS GOOD AS NEW
HAPPY NEW YEAR
OUR LAST SUMMER
SLIPPING THROUGH MY FINGERS
LIKE AN ANGEL PASSING THROUGH MY ROOM
PUT ON YOUR WHITE SOMBRERO

MAMMA MIA! THE MOVIE SOUNDTRACK
HONEY, HONEY" - AMANDA SEYFRIED, ASHLEY LILLEY &
RACHEL MCDOWALL
MONEY, MONEY, MONEY" - MERYL STREEP, JULIE WALTERS
& CHRISTINE BARANSKI
MAMMA MIA" - MERYL STREEP
DANCING QUEEN" - MERYL STREEP, JULIE WALTERS &
CHRISTINE BARANSKI
OUR LAST SUMMER" - COLIN FIRTH, PIERCE BROSNAN,
STELLAN SKARSGÅRD, MERYL STREEP & AMANDA SEYFRIED
LAY ALL YOUR LOVE ON ME" - DOMINIC COOPER &
AMANDA SEYFRIED
SUPER TROUPER" - MERYL STREEP, JULIE WALTERS &
CHRISTINE BARANSKI
GIMME! GIMME! GIMME! (A MAN AFTER MIDNIGHT)" –
AMANDA SEYFRIED, ASHLEY LILLEY & RACHEL MCDOWALL
THE NAME OF THE GAME" - AMANDA SEYFRIED
VOULEZ-VOUS" - FULL CAST, PHILIP MICHAEL, CHRISTINE
BARANSKI, JULIE WALTERS & STELLAN SKARSGÅRD
SOS" - PIERCE BROSNAN & MERYL STREEP
DOES YOUR MOTHER KNOW" - CHRISTINE BARANSKI &
PHILIP MICHAEL
SLIPPING THROUGH MY FINGERS" - MERYL STREEP &
AMANDA SEYFRIED

THE WINNER TAKES IT ALL" - MERYL STREEP
WHEN ALL IS SAID AND DONE" - PIERCE BROSNAN &
MERYL STREEP
TAKE A CHANCE ON ME" - JULIE WALTERS, STELLAN
SKARSGÅRD, COLIN FIRTH, PHILIP MICHAEL & CHRISTINE
BARANSKI
I HAVE A DREAM"/"THANK YOU FOR THE MUSIC" (HIDDEN
TRACK) - AMANDA SEYFRIED

BIBLIOGRAHY

THE FOLLOWING ALBUMS WERE FOUND ON:
http://www.abba-story.com/albums.html
THE DEFINITIVE COLLECTION
ORO - GRANDES EXITOS
MORE ABBA GOLD
ABBA GOLD
ABBA LIVE
THE SINGLES - THE FIRST TEN YEARS
THE VISITORS
GRACIAS POR LA MUSICAL
SUPER TROUPER
VOULEZ-VOUS
GREATEST HITS VOL. II
ABBA - THE ALBUM
ARRIVAL
ABBA
GREATEST HITS
WATERLOO
RING RING

THE FOLLOWING ALBUMS WERE FOUND ON:
http://en.wikipedia.org/wiki/The_Best_of_ABBA
18 HITS
ABBA LIVE
THANK YOU FOR THE MUSIC (ALBUM)
THE COMPLETE STUDIO RECORDINGS (ABBA ALBUM)
DVD 1 THE VIDEOS
DVD 2 THE HISTORY
LIVE IN APRIL 1981
SINGLES
MAMMA MIA! THE MOVIE SOUNDTRACK

ABOUT THE AUTHOR

I was 59 years old; a mother of three very special and supportive adult children and a grandmother of three wonderful grandsons (I now have five grand-children.) when I started writing my first book whilst watching a Bon Jovi concert DVD. (I am an avid fan, if you can call me that; crazy is more like it.)

I write from the heart and I really enjoyed writing the book so I wrote another using a different artist, and the books kept coming to me and I kept writing them.(with a little help from above)

Because I use different artist/artists song titles I have to be very careful with Copyright so a lot of legal requirements have to be taken into consideration before publishing the books. I also needed a name that would connect my books to each other; so the "Song Title Series" books began.

All my books are short stories; however it depends on how many song titles there are to be used, as to the length of the book. Some artists didn't have enough song titles on their own so I combined them with a few other artists. Other artists had that many song titles that I could have written a novel; but it would have ended up being boring.

Challenges I like, so writing books with various artists are a lot of fun and require careful thinking.

Why should I have all the fun writing the books and not be able to share them with everyone; so I have converted them into large print books so that you can share my fun as well.

Hopefully in the not too distant future; the books will also be available as audio books so that no-one will miss out on my fun and enjoyment of writing these unique books. I hope that you enjoy reading them.

My web site www.songtitleseries.com is the place to visit for updates of new books and a place to purchase other titles in other formats.

TESTIMONIALS

After reading through your range of books I felt I must compliment you Joan on the imaginative and entertaining way in which you presented each group and the Musicians in those groups. The way the stories were constructed is a credit to your work ethic. These must have taken considerable time to piece together and it is obviously a work of love for you.
I wish you all the success you truly deserve and look forward to seeing you next time you visit Tamworth.
Peter Harkins
Managing Director Cheapa Music
Country Music Capital Tamworth

The song titles series are books that were intriguing and were hard to believe that these short stories were written within the incorporated song titles of the artists that are mentioned in the titles. I loved what I have read so far and think that anyone with an imagination and love of music as the author you will surely enjoy reading these.   L.K. Brisbane Australia.

Joan Maguire Books are very nice, I enjoy reading them so much, they are hard to put down!! Especially when she does one about Bonjovi and their songs!!!
If I can say, it is worth every penny, when you buy one!!! The Books make nice presents, for a person whom loves to read!!! I can guarantee that you will LOVE these books, because I do!!!!!!!!!
Dawn from Newark, Delaware in the United States of America

I am Susie and would like to tell you guys, how much I am enjoying Joan Maguire's Books!! They are very enjoyable, and they are something that you do not ever want to put down!! I really enjoy these books; I can't wait until the next one that she puts out!!!!!!! I say go to your local book store, today and get one, you will not be disappointed!!!!!
Sue-from the United States of America